THE WATERS OF DONEGAL

SHORT STORIES

DANIEL MacCARRON

D.M.C. UNIVERSAL, LIMITED
South Circular Road
Islandbridge
Dublin

Dedication:

This book is dedicated to the memory of my uncles and aunts, namely, Kate Shovelin, John and Edward MacGowan, Jimmy Gallagher, Kate MacElwee, Jim and Owen MacCarron, John Crerand, Hugh and Bridget MacDaid, Eddy and Ellen MacBride and Eamon O'Sullivan — R.I.P.

Acknowledgements:

I thank the following: Fr Eugene MacDermot, Geraldine O'Connor, Ann Doyle, Anne Foley and others, including the tutors of the B.A. School of Successful Writing, who read and criticised some of these stories; Helen Foran who helped with the Art Work; and all who in any way helped the writing and preparation of this book for publication.

I hope that all who read this book will enjoy it as much as I enjoyed writing it for their entertainment.

DANIEL MacCARRON

Carrodoan P.O.,
Letterkenny,
County Donegal.
August 26, 1982.

First published 1982
by D.M.C. Universal, Limited,
751 South Circular Road,
Dublin 8,
Ireland.
Telephone 718424
Typeset by Fingerprint.
Printed and bound in England by
Billing & Sons Limited,
Worcester.
ISBN 0 9507808 3 9

CONTENTS

THE SALDANHA DISASTER IN LOUGH SWILLY

As 1814 dawned, Europe's war with Napoleon entered a critical phase. The once invincible armies of that great military genius were being pushed gradually but steadily back towards the boundaries of Revolutionary France. With each new Allied success, whether real or apparent, another government would openly denounce him and take the field against him at the side of his adversaries. As huge numbers of enemy troops massed on the French frontier for a final assault on his Empire, the people of France — at last weary of war and realising the hopelessness of their country's military position — listlessly awaited the invasion of their country and the defeat of their man of destiny.

Two years earlier, in peaceful Ireland, far from the horrors of the Napoleonic war, a group of battleships belonging to the Royal Navy lay at anchor in Lough Swilly, County Donegal.

November, 1811, was an exceptional month: The skies were clear, and the sun shone with an unusual warmth for that time of the year. While these ships, and their crews, were basking in this serene and peaceful atmosphere, a despatch from the Admiralty arrived at naval headquarters, in Buncrana.

This despatch contained an order of vast importance for many people — in short, the Admiralty was ordering the Saldanha and her sister ship to sail to the Bay of Biscay. They were instructed to put troops ashore at a specific Spanish port and to cannonade the French Emperor's coastal fortifications in the region of the Pyrenees.

Little is known about her sister ship but the Saldanha was

a 5th Rate 36 guns 145 x 39 ft. battleship, built at South Shields and launched on December 8, 1809. Her Captain was the Honorable William Packenham.

Buncrana was bustling with activity during the last days of the month; troops, for embarkation, were pouring into the town from barracks in the City of Derry and from forts along the Foyle and Swilly; merchants and quarter-masters were busy putting munitions, stores and provisions on board the two ships being fitted out for the long, dangerous voyage.

As anticipated, the month of December came in clear and very calm. All day, on December 3, the crews of the two ships waited patiently for a favourable wind; towards dusk a slight breeze began to blow from the direction of Moville. Slowly, the Saldanha and her sister ship set sail down Lough Swilly.

The troops on board these ships were in high spirits and looking forward to doing battle with Bonaparte; nevertheless they were lonely leaving Donegal, and their loved ones, since the Holy season of Christmas was near at hand; but they sang patriotic songs and, as they strolled on deck to keep warm, they watched — with emotion and interest — lights being lit in the forts, cabins and villages, on the shorelands; and on ships and fishing-boats in the harbour. They stayed on deck until the temperature dropped and the lights went out of sight; then, obeying orders, they berthed for the night and went to sleep.

The Saldanha and her sister ship were not more than a dozen miles beyond the mouth of the Lake of Shadows, which is a complimentary name for Lough Swilly, when the wind changed direction and increased in strength. Then, quite suddenly, it became a gale, tossing these ships about like corks, breaking their canvas and causing the troops on board to become violently sick.

Captain Packenham, fearing the worst if his beloved ship were to continue sailing through the terrible Atlantic in such a dreadful tempest, shouted above the noise of the winds, and the excited voices of his busy crew, to the Captain of the sister ship.

"Sir, it is my intention to return to the safety of Lough Swilly. What are your plans?"

3 The Waters of Donegal

These two gallant and expert seamen were in an appalling dilemma. After some thought, the Captain of the other ship replied:

"I quite understand sir. To return to harbour was my first impulse when this . . . rather nasty gale blew up . . . but in view of the urgency of the Admiralty's communication to headquarters five days ago, and what I consider to be a rather lengthy delay in our sailing, I have ordered my ship to continue on course to the Bay of Biscay. I shall not rescind this order . . . In any event, I suppose, you and I will have to do our duty, old boy, what, what . . .?"

Their conversation ended at this point because of the noise of the gale and the growing distance between their ships.

The two ships parted company off Fanad Head. The Saldanha, while returning to Buncrana, was driven off course in the dark by the gale and the raging swell. She struck Swilly Rock early on the morning of December 4, sank, pulling down with her all on board except one sailor, who swam through the mountainous waves to the shore on the Fanad Peninsula, where he died soon afterwards from exhaustion and exposure.

Unsteady of posture and blurred in speech, this man's last words to fishermen, who had gathered on shore to render assistance to survivors, were:

"Men, it was a terrible night!"

Then he collapsed.

An Epic was written some time after the disaster to tell the story of the ill-fated ship and to perpetuate the memory of her nameless hero. The poem was later set to music and became a beautiful lyric. The composer is unknown but it is reasonable to suppose that he was born on the Banks of Lough Swilly and was a fisherman by profession. To this day whenever and wherever Lough Swilly fishermen are gathered together, and a song is requested, one of them is sure to sing the Ballad of the Saldanha.

THE SALDANHA

Come all you Lough Swilly seamen,
    And listen to my song;

Pay heed unto this tragedy,
   I will not keep you long:
It's of the Talbot Sloop-of-war,
   The Saldanha also;
On the Third Day of December,
   These ships to sea did go.

On the Fourth Day of December,
   The wind began to blow —
It strongly blew from the North-East
   With heavy squalls of snow;
The great tempest still continued,
   The Talbot bore to sea;
But brave Saldanha and her men
   Sailed for Lough Swilly lee.

The wind shifted into the North,
   How dismal was the night;
It was at Fanad's Signal-Pole
   That we observed a light.
But at the hour of six o'clock
   That light we saw no more;
And at the third watch of the night,
   We ran aground on shore!

Helpless was our situation —
   No mercy from the waves,
Which soon did wreck our gallant ship,
   The seas became our graves.
Yet one man out of three hundred,
   Those cruel waves did withstand,
He swam alive unto the shore,
   And died on Stocker Strand!

A SPOT OF WHITEWASHING

Two friends sat drinking together in a public house on the sea-front. They were in their late forties. One of the men was very thin, and tall, with a pale complexion, and had a high, bald, forehead; the other man was of medium height, heavy set, with a red face. He was wearing a hat and had it thrust far back on his large, round head.

Many years had passed since their last meeting, and because of this they had much to discuss; they were, therefore, so engrossed in the task at hand that they paid scant attention to their surroundings and did not notice Benedict O'Connell, when he entered the lounge-bar and made his way to the counter.

Benedict made a sign to the publican and ordered a bottle of stout. While waiting for his drink to be served Benedict put his left elbow on the counter in a casual manner, as was his way, and, turning half-way round, looked down the full length of the room; he pushed his cap back on the side of his head and wiped the perspiration off his forehead with his right palm.

It was at this point that one of the friends recognised Benedict. Turning to his companion, he whispered something in the latter's ear; the latter turned about instantly to look at the man standing at the counter.

The publican delivered the drink to Benedict. Benedict, turning back to face the publican, took change from his pocket and handed it to him, and said:

"Thanks Paddy. You might as well give me twenty Players while you are at it."

The publican nodded.

"Man dear, Benny! How are you doing?" the tall man said, loudly. "We did not know you when you came in just now. How are you at all? Still sledging away on the land?"

At first Benedict was startled. Then, he recognised the husky voice.

"Camillus MacClusky is it?" he exclaimed joyously, and reaching for his drink, and cigarettes, moved shyly but rapidly over to join the two friends. At their invitation he sat down in a chair near their table, and drawing a deep breath, said excitedly: "Camillus! — as sure as God above in Heaven, I did not know you; I saw you sitting there, chatting to this fellow, when I came in. But from Adam I did not know you. You have changed! Man dear! — if you had not spoken, I would have walked right out that door again without speaking to you, and you would think I had a grudge against you, so you would surely."

"O'Connell, I am glad to meet you again," the man with the round head said, extending a huge hand in greeting.

Benedict took the hand of the stranger and looked him over with blank dismay. The man shook Benedict's hand vigorously, obviously delighted to see him. The stranger, noticing Benedict's disadvantage, spoke in a subdued tone:

"I am Richard O'Corrigan who used to be hired, years ago, with old Maxwell MacClure, in Kildonalbane, next door to Camillus here."

"Ara begod I know you now," Benedict said with genuine feeling. "You were a bloody good runner, and footballer — if I remember rightly — and a hard man."

"He was that too and all," Camillus confirmed solemnly. "And did you never have the pleasure of hearing him sing? He could sing a verse or two as good as the next fellow, so he could."

Benedict was, once again, perplexed.

"Maybe I did," Benedict muttered, disappointed that he could not recall having heard Richard sing. "That would be over twenty years since you were working for MacClure, if it is a day," he said at last, apologetically. "But one thing I do remember, you were the best right-forward I ever did see play in my young days, so you were, indeed. Did you follow it up after you left Kildonalbane?"

"Damn the bit of me," Richard replied, despondently. "When you are digging sewer-drains through the streets of Glasgow, seven days of the week, and married to a Scots woman, you soon drop your daft notions about playing football. You have not got the time nor the energy. You learn sense and —"

"That is true and all," Camillus agreed.

Benedict thought he noticed a spark of regret in Richard's voice regarding football, and he decided to change the subject. "What are you fellows having?" he asked with enthusiasm.

"We were about to leave, and have a quiet stroll through the regatta, to see what we could see, and who we could see, and have a long chat about old times. But damn it all, we shall let you stand us a drink for old time's sake," Camillus replied, looking at Richard for his support.

Richard nodded his consent. "Make mine a small Black & White."

When their drinks were placed before them Richard asked Benedict about MacClure's health. Benedict told him MacClure was ill in hospital, and that Mrs MacClure, who was a bit odd in ways, was carrying on the running of their farm on her own — neither seeking nor accepting help from her neighbours.

"What is the matter with MacClure?" Richard asked anxiously. Adding: "He was an honest man all his day. He might want plenty of work done but he was a decent Presbyterian. Honest men are rare these days — hard to find really honest men. Mind you, I would like to see him again before I return to Glasgow . . . Mrs MacClure — there is a woman for you! She was always peculiar — never said much, just kept looking at you or through you, yet, saying nothing much. I could not size her up; a strange woman surely. O'Connell, tell me about MacClure; what is wrong with his health? — I would like to know?"

Richard took a sip of whisky and looked earnestly at Benedict.

"MacClure," Benedict began, "was in the pick of health until last May. Now he is in the mental —"

"The mental! You mean to say he is in the asylum?"

Richard asked, astonished. "He was a sensible man all his days. The only thing he could not understand was my playing football on Sundays — you know how strict Protestants around here are about doing things of that nature on the Sabbath —"

"Well, he is in the mental asylum, all right," Benedict repeated, and continued: "Not mad, really; more confused than any thing else. I shall tell you the whole story."

Benedict pulled the cap forward on his head and made a gesture with his stout glass and began with gusto:

"Mrs MacClure has a sister, called Betty Ann, living in Canada. Last April she got a letter from Canada telling her that Betty Ann and two nieces were coming to Ireland for a holiday and would be staying with her for a couple of weeks in July. The Mrs asked old MacClure to tidy up their steading and give the outhouses a splash of whitewash into the bargain.

"The way I heard it, MacClure told her whitewashing was not his trade; that he was a farmer — not a painter. She kept on, and on, about the whitewashing, until, for peacesake, he whitewashed the dwelling house and a few of the outhouses. She was in the best of humour with him, then. He ran out of lime before he had the houses finished and ordered a bag of gaslime to complete the job. When he had all the outhouses whitewashed, he started on the stone ditches and rocks around and about their farm."

Richard and Camillus were listening intently.

"Next, MacClure ordered a lorry-load of gaslime. Mrs MacClure did not twig, at first, what was up — she thought he was thinking of building some new outhouse or an extension to their dwelling-house. Sure that was not his idea at all. The man was going mad!

"MacClure started whitewashing the streets and lanes on his farm; he even did a long stretch of the country road. The Surveyors and the Guards came to see him about this carry-on. I believe they had had a load of trouble convincing him that, under no circumstances whatsoever, was he to put whitewash on the public roads. So, he switched to whitewashing the roofs and all the machinery, tools and furniture in and about their home.

"Until he started whitewashing the bushes and trees and animals on their farm, Mrs MacClure was not sure whether he was joking or in earnest — it was at this point that she asked me one evening in June, to call on Dr O'Broligan, to tell him what MacClure was doing, and to get the doctor's advice. Sure! — once Dr O'Broligan heard me out, he knew what was wrong. Says he to me: 'O'Connell, tell Mrs MacClure, when you return home that I am going out her way on my rounds in the afternoon and shall call on her and see what I can do for Mr MacClure'.

"And sure enough, he told her MacClure was in need of treatment for his nerves and had him committed, the same evening, to the district asylum —"

"Will he come all right in the end?" Richard asked, concernedly.

"I believe so," Benedict replied. "The doctor told Mrs. MacClure not to worry, that there was a similar case reported in England two years ago, and that that patient — also a farmer — was discharged, as right as rain, less than six months after his entry to the mental clinic."

"The mind is a funny thing," Richard said philosophically.

"It is too and all," Camillus confirmed with gravity. "It is very delicate; a delicate piece of mechanism, surely."

Benedict looked at his glass, gestured again, shook his head knowingly, and said solemnly:

"Ach! Sure if it was known, maybe none of us is too square in the head — there is always some thing wrong with a body; if it is not one thing, it is another —"

"Could be some thing that is in gaslime which goes to the brain," Richard speculated with candour.

Benedict nodded and rearranged his cap. "It could well be, Richard," he replied. "It seems curious but why does it happen to farmers?"

"You had better stay away from whitewashing," Camillus told Benedict. "I am going to think twice before I do a spot of whitewashing for the Mrs. in future. It is very funny when you come to think of it that way, too and all," Camillus added, bursting out laughing.

Benedict saw the funny side of it and joined in Camillus' hilarity, and, for a long while, the two of them were rocking with laughter.

Richard did not join them however. He entertained a personal liking for MacClure, regarding him almost as dearly as one would a favourite uncle. He did not consider MacClure's whitewashing obsession any thing at which to laugh, as did the other two.

"We should be going for that stroll now," he suggested fiercely, getting to his feet, abruptly.

Seeing Richard's annoyance, Benedict and Camillus stopped laughing.

"You are not angry at us for laughing, are you Richard?" Benedict said, observing Richard's solemnity. "I always thought highly of Maxwell MacClure. I was not laughing at him personally but at his strange affliction; it is so unusual – no disrespect meant; and I am sure the same goes for Camillus here?"

"It does too and all," Camillus confirmed with feigned seriousness.

They left the public-house in silence. When they were on the pavement, on the opposite side of the street, Richard turned to his companions, and spoke quietly and gravely:

"The day I left MacClure's service nineteen years ago come next November, I told him I was going to try my luck in Scotland. He told me he thought I was a good, honest worker, and he assured me he regretted losing my services. As I was getting into the taxi, that was to take me to the Derry-boat, he slipped me a tenner. Says he:

" 'That sum of money might come in very handy on the streets of Glasgow'!

"And do you know something? He was correct!"

Benedict and Camillus looked at each other as Richard continued:

"Shortly after landing in Scotland I became violently ill and thought I was going to die, I was very sick; to the pesent day I am not sure what was the matter, but, as sure as there is salt-water in the Swilly, that £10 note saved my life! You know what I mean, men?"

"It beats all," Benedict exclaimed, considering it a revelation.

"It does too and all," Camillus agreed, and scratched his

bald head.

There were tears in Richard's eyes as he and his two companions walked slowly and silently down the street towards the regatta!

THE THIRSTY SAILORS

An English merchant ship anchored in Lough Swilly during a storm.

When the storm abated, but before the ship resumed her voyage to the Clyde, a small boat was launched and four members of the ship's crew rowed ashore for refreshments.

The sailors landed on the Fanad Peninsula at Bunnaton. They pulled the little boat to the high water mark and began to walk up the sand dunes.

When they had walked a few hundred yards over the road, one of them, who was very talkative, said:

"Beautiful valley, mates."

They stood and looked about them and agreed that the valley was truly beautiful and serene.

"I wonder how far it is to the nearest public house?" said the talkative sailor to his companions.

They were working up a terrific thirst from walking fast and from thinking about drink as they continued up the Glen.

When they had walked over a quarter of a mile they met old Alfy Tinney. Says the talkative sailor to Alfy:

"What's the name of this valley?"

Alfy's knowledge of English was skanty. He did not understand what the word 'valley' meant. But he managed to say:

"Come again."

The talkative sailor gestured. "What's this glen called, mate?"

Alfy understood what the sailor was trying to say: "This is Glenvar, A Chara."

"Thanks mate,' but my name is George, not a chara."

The Glenman smiled.

"Say, where's the nearest public house, mate?" George asked.

Alfy had heard the term 'public house' once or twice before but he could not recall what it meant exactly, but not wanting to appear stupid, and prepared to take a chance that the meaning was 'public toilet', he replied earnestly:

"Ara, go into the park there," he said and pointed to the high stone wall and the field behind it, and pub away, the coleens no see ye."

Seeing that Alfy had misunderstood, George, winking to his companions, said·

"Thank you, awfully, mate, you have been most helpful, what?"

"Bannacht libh," replied Alfy; then he moved on up the hill for a load of turf with his donkey and cart.

The sailors continued their walk for about another quarter of a mile before meeting James Crerand coming over the road with a load of hay on his horse and cart.

"How far is it to the nearest village?" George put to James.

"Kerrykeel would be the nearest village?" James speculated; he pointed up the Glen. "The village is on the other side of that hill. Cross over, go down to Mulroy Bay, and just before you reach the water, there is the town of Kerrykeel, men."

"Thanks mate," said George gratefully. "Say, how far is it?"

"I always heard it said that the journey from the bottom of the Glen to Loughrey's Corner in Kerrykeel was five miles. A right long walk, men," said James and he led the horse and the load of hay down a side road.

"Thanks again, mate," George shouted above the noise of the cart and James' whistle. Then to his mates: "That was a decent chap. I'd say we have four miles to go, what? If we lift our feet at the double, we can be in a public house within the hour. Blamey, come, let's get a move on, I'm over-board for a beer and a woman, mates," and with those inspiring words the four sailors began to march in military style up the Glen towards Kerrykeel.

Just beyond the chapel, where the road branches off towards the townland of Creeve, stood Joe Logue's forge. Outside, men waited to have their horses shod. Seeing them, and not knowing which road to take, George left his companions standing at the cross-roads and ran up to the forge to seek directions.

"Which road, and how far is it to Kerrykeel, mate?" George asked one of the men. George was out of breath after his sprint.

The men eyed him suspiciously. George was the first sailor they had ever seen in Glenvar, and his presence set them wondering. None of them spoke to him. Instead they looked from one to the other and at George. Then one of them shouted:

"Joe, come out here a minute, there's a sailor looking for directions to Kerrykeel."

Joe came out of the forge wearing his apron and holding a hammer in one hand and a horse shoe in the other. Since he had worked in Derry City during the war, and had been one of Spider Kelly's sparring partners, the men thought he was qualified to handle the sailor with the wild eyes, long nose, and scared face.

Joe, who had met sailors of every nationality in Derry City, told the sailor which road led to Kerrykeel: "The village is five miles up the other road . . ."

George returned to his companions. "The Blacksmith told us to keep straight on over that hill," George told them and pointed to the South. "The sky is looking like pissing, mates, we had better hurry."

About a mile further on they met a stout man with a pick-axe and a shovel coming down the road riding a bicycle. His Christian name was Paddy. He was employed by the County Council as a 'surfaceman'. Says George to the workman:

"A minute, mate, how far is it from here to Kerrykeel?"

Paddy got off the bicycle. "Are you going to the town?" Paddy, who had not heard the sailor properly, asked.

"Aye, aye, mate; how far is it to Kerrykeel? Are we on the right road, what?" George asked anxiously.

"You're on the right road sure enough," said Paddy kindly. He was stout and wore a hat. "I'd safely say you've five miles to go. Good luck, men." Leaving the sailors standing, wondering, Paddy peddled down the road towards the next pothole or blocked watermain.

The sailors had walked three miles. No wonder they were confused. "Five miles to Kerrykeel from the bottom of the Glen, five miles to Kerrykeel from the top of the Glen," George put to his companions good humouredly; "keep going, mates, you're holding your own!"

Puzzled still, the sailors walked on at a frisky pace over the hill and reached the village before the rain began to fall heavily. They entered a public house, where Hughie Shields told them to their amusement, that country people speak very loosely of distance, and that in any event there were two measures in use in Ireland, namely, the Irish Mile and the English or Statute Mile. When these factors were explained to them, and they were assured that the Glenmen did not confuse them on purpose, they laughed at the misunderstanding, and George bought drinks for everybody.

DONEGAL'S ANCIENT REPUBLIC

Long ago, when Donegal was still a Republic, there lived a crank by the name of Peto MacMurray. Entirely lacking in moderation, he was a rather religious, politically ambitious woodcutter of average education and abilities.

From the day he was old enough to understand politics, Peto was a fanatical follower of the fiercely patriotic Conservation Party; but with the passage of time, and the availability of enlightened literature on the black market, he switched his support to a new party by the name of the Liberality Party.

The Liberality Party intended to break new ground, to put theories into practice, and to reform the monetary and taxation systems; and it began by making or endeavouring to make a large appeal to all sections of the community by advocating radical policies in order to bring unemployment under control and to prevent emigration to the island of New Siberia.

Shortly after joining the new party, by the fair force of hard work and enthusiasm for this political association, and the Liberality Party having few party hacks and fervent followers as yet, Peto was put in charge of its propaganda department. Furthermore, he obtained the party's nomination for election to parliament. This was not at all difficult because political opportunists of a wiser vintage refused to accept nominations for fear of losing their deposits and electable reputations. But true to form Peto let these alleged honours go to his head and he became more hard-working and loyal to the Liberality Party than ever before; he began to think of himself as an influential person and as a future government minister.

As part of his job as propaganda chief of the Liberality Party, Peto wrote letters to the editors of all the leading Donegal newspapers of the day, and published leaflets and booklets expounding the aims and policies of the party. He did not lack courage. He was not shy about expressing his personal views. Whether as an ordinary citizen (expressing his views) or as a party propaganda chief advocating radical politics, Peto's press releases were always adroitly, solidly, and attractively presented. His opponents reluctantly but privately conceded as much and they regretted that someone so sincere and able wasted his time and talents trying to promote a party without the least chance of success; yet his ideas began to permeate their thinking; and in spite of their claim that he was flogging a dead donkey they were genuinely worried that the Liberality Party would win from themselves much financial and electoral support.

Peto resented the Conservation Party more strongly than any other party because it had not given him a nomination while he was its member. He disliked the crooked land deals made by some of its leading politicians. He was delighted when it lost the election to the Rightus and Leftus parties, who had agreed to fight the election jointly and to form an 'Alternative Coalition' government if a majority of their candidates was elected to parliament. But the government formed by these parties, despite some fine reforms, failed to increase economic prosperity to any satisfactory level. It proved to be financially extravagant. It also displeased the uncommitted citizen through its security and welfare arrangements. And many citizens, who, having forgotten the rotten land and contract deals of the Conservation Party politicians, began to call on voters to shift their support from the Alternative Coalition back to the Conservation Party. He did not particularly like the Rightus Party for having executed, by bow and arrow, some of his childhood heroes in a civil war and he was wary of the Leftus Party because of its pronounced anti-religious bias. However, fearing a return to power of the Conservationists, whom he loathed because of their dishonest and vacillating politics, Peto was forced — most against the grain — to defend the record of the Alternative Coalition, while hoping at the same time that his own party would be returned to power, but until it did he wanted to see the Conservation Party continued in opposition.

The Conservation Party, seeing that the Rightus and Leftus parties looked like retaining control of the government for an indefinite period, appointed a hack-writer by the name of Emo MacFrank to spearhead its attack upon the personnel and political actions of the Alternative Coalition.

MacFrank, who was a butler by trade, proved to be such an adept political writer that his letters attacking the performance of the Alternative Coalition government, and published in the Lough Swilly Echo, Glencolmcille Observer and Cranford Chronicle, actually began to win wide support for the Conservation Party. Peto became alarmed. True to character he wrote letters of refutation. But still support for the despised Conservation Party continued to grow larger by the day. At this point Peto decided to take a gamble: He would compose a piece of satire in order to discredit the political mentality of Emo MacFrank and coax citizens into voting for his own Liberality Party candidacy. This is what he wrote subject to editorial correction:

"The wit contained in Emo MacFrank's letters as published in your newspaper over a period of six months amused me and, I suppose, many of your other readers enjoyed too this form of cheap entertainment since otherwise you would not have printed them in your widely read weekly.

In all of his writings Emo criticised the government and praised the opposition. He was true to his name when he frankly admitted having voted for the Leftus and Rightus parties at the last election for the sake of change. Now he greatly regrets his folly, he says, and advises voters to support next time the Conservation Party.

Being young and inexperienced, impulsive, hard-working and well-meaning, Emo, who has a short memory, is anxious to help his compatriots avoid committing the same folly; this is the core of his messages, I believe.

I would caution Emo against being too concerned, for all of us have made mistakes in the past: I was once a member of the Conservation Party. But my mistake and Emo's mistake are trivial when compared with the dilemma faced some years ago by an innocent chamber maid. Feeling faint in the mornings she went to see a physician. After the good doctor had completed his examination, he told his attractive patient: 'I am afraid Miss Fado that you are pregnant!' Sure his youthful but foolish patient was flabbergasted until she recalled the proverb: 'Doctors differ and patients die.' 'Do not be supercilious,' she told him indignantly. 'If I have made a mistake, what so? Who has not made a few mistakes during his life?' The doctor did not reply because he knew she spoke factually. From that day forward Miss Fado's admonition to all virgins, was: 'Keep away from fellahs!' Like that foolish maiden, Emo has been gullible and therefore made a grave political error at the last election, or so he claims. But he must be careful, however, lest perhaps he commit a far greater error in advising others to vote for the opposition. Extreme positions like Miss Fado's must be avoided. I shall relate a short anecdote for his benefit:

"Once upon a time two brothers, Emo and Peto, lived on a small low-lying farm in the North East part of our Republic. Emo owned a jackass and Peto owned a mule. The brothers lived by selling vegetables and turf in the capital city. With the ass and cart Emo made four trips weekly to the city, the ass carrying four bags of vegetables per load and doing the journey in four hours; Peto's mule, carrying eight bags of turf per load, took three hours to do the trip twice weekly.

"No one, excepting Peto, liked the mule because it was a little lame and was extremely sombre; yet it was a sturdy animal, a willing worker, and always behaved itself in the best manner of its breed. Whereas the ass was shifty, lazy, crafty, and a great favourite with the ladies because it roared elegantly and winked at them in a very romantic manner.

"One day an elderly lady said to Peto: 'Why do you not sell that dreadful-looking mule and buy a nice friendly donkey like the animal Emo has?'

"Peto was slightly upset at this talk but being a gentleman, who hated to hurt people's feelings, he replied politely nevertheless: 'Thank you most kindly, Madam, for your solicitude. You see,' he went on patiently to explain to the foolish lady, 'I require an animal capable of taking a large load of turf, Madam, and an ass would carry less and take longer to complete a trip to market.' 'Nonsense, Peto,' the lady interjected with some passion, 'Emo's donkey is so lovable, lively, and such a sweet dear, that I am sure Emo is making just as much profit for the business as you are making with that ugly beast you call a mule.' Peto defended his honourable mule, and replied: 'Quite the contrary, my mule is economical and dependable despite appearances. In any event, Madam, our business is practically a non-profit making organisation, as we barely make a poor living —' 'Still and all,' the cultured but ignorant lady said pertly, 'I would rather have the donkey any day.'

By making insinuations the lady instilled doubts in Peto's mind, and as he travelled homewards he debated with himself the proposition: 'Should he sell the mule and buy an ass so as to please some of the customers?' He grew so excited as he walked along, and spoke so loudly about his love of the mule and his disgust with little lazy donkeys, that the Blacksmith came out to ask him what was the matter as he passed the forge. He opened his heart and confused mind to the smith. 'If I were you, Peto, I would sell the donkey and mule and buy myself a young, healthy Clydesdale,' said the smith authoritively. 'Sure the horse would take the vegetables and turf to the capital city in one load and do the trip in two hours. Never be swayed by the foolish talk of ignorant people so long as you give the public a good service, I always say,' the smith added earnestly.

The brothers took the Blacksmith's advice, sold the donkey and mule, bought the horse, and died millionaires.

The mule and donkey represent the government and opposition respectively; the farm is the sovereign Republic of Donegal; the brothers are the voters; the lady is the foolish political hack writer; the horse is the Liberality Party; and the Blacksmith is myself, Peto MacMurray, the wise citizen.

The moral of the anecdote is this: 'We must elect the candidates of the Liberality Party and get rid of the candidates of the Conservation, Rightus and Leftus parties at the next election, as it is obvious to all right-thinking citizens that these parties do not meet the requirements of the time.'

The publication of that letter of Peto MacMurray caused a public outcry against himself and his party; he was threatened with law suits; the editors of all the newspapers that printed his letter resigned in disgrace when legal proceedings were brought against their newspapers for immoral and inflammatory publishing. Legal proceedings were dropped or suspended when the newspaper companies agreed to pay the injured parties nominal damages and expenses and promised most solemnly never again to publish any of the political polemics or literary works of Peto MacMurray.

Peto was asked by his party colleagues to resign his parliamentary nomination and to step down as the propaganda chief of the Liberality Party. They were afraid he would bring political ruin to the party. They went so far as to issue a public rebuke and to disassociate themselves from his letter's sentiments. But the harm was done: The Liberality Party did not succeed in having one of its one thousand odd candidates elected to parliament. It eventually became defunct. Peto went forward himself in the election as an independent but was decisively rejected by the electorate; disheartened, he retired from public life, and nothing was heard of him again. No doubt he had learned that satire was not a popular way to promote a new political movement in the Republic's conservative society. The Liberality Party and Peto were far ahead of their time. This was borne out by the fact that, from then until the end of the Republic's life, the Conservation and Alternative Coalition parties continued to hold power — on and off — despite the effects of new political parties to oust them.

The repressive and inept Republic went down to defeat and slavery when fierce fighting tribes from the island of Rochall invaded Donegal about the year 1324 B.C.

THE YOUNG DOCTOR

The wind blew the curtains across the room. From the open window the entire sweep of Sheephaven Bay was visible. Perched on a height in a neighbouring field stood a proud, large, well-fed, grey donkey watching the curtains waving in the window.

The young Doctor placed his medical case on the little table at the window. When he had addressed his patient he opened the case; and as he looked at the Bay his eye caught sight of the donkey.

"Who owns the donkey, Peter?" he asked the patient.

The patient, who was smoking his pipe against the young Doctor's orders, sat up in bed and put the pipe on the table. "You mean that big grey donkey in the rocky field to the left of the house, Doctor?"

"Yes," replied the young Doctor. "It is a fine specimen."

"That is Deeney's Jackass," said the patient without interest.

"He seems to be an intelligent, strong, and well-cared for beast," continued the young Doctor as he placed a thermometer in the patient's mouth and placed the stethescope on his chest. Later he said: "Deep breath, please."

The patient, who was an old Fisherman, did as he was commanded and soon the examination was at an end.

"No change," the young Doctor announced more to himself than to the old Fisherman as he put his instruments away and took a small box of pills from his medical case and put it on the table beside the still smoulding pipe. He was tired telling the old Fisherman to give up smoking because it was bad for cancer. The old Fisherman always said he would try his best. As often he would say with conviction:

"Aye, I'll try but I won't guarantee. Sure, I'm as old as I am and smoking hasn't killed me yet." And the young Doctor, whose patience was rather short of late because of an increased demand for his services, would try to speak in an even, pleading tone of voice when saying:

"Smoking is not helping your Condition, Peter."

It was two years since the young Doctor came to the district and most people wished him to remain because of his skill and attention to duty. The old Fisherman, who was suffering from pains in his bowels and from frequent attacks of diarrhoea, knew that his was an incurable disease because otherwise the young Doctor would have had him as right as rain long ago or would have referred him to a specialist in the local district hospital. The young Doctor was tight-lipped about what was wrong with his patient, but the old Fisherman wanted to drag a true opinion out of him one way or the other. He had been saying:

"Do you think it's piles I have, Doctor? Do you think I'll soon be back fishing? Do you think I've the bug (meaning cancer of the bowels)?"

But the young Doctor would not give him any satisfaction. Always he was evasive. This, more than anything else, showed that the old Fisherman was far from well, and he felt that he was slowly but steadily going down hill, and he genuinely wanted to know what it was that was gradually beating the life out of him and preventing his return to the Bay and to the fishing.

In spite of his sufferings the old Fisherman was always good humoured and witty. The young Doctor, who was often the butt of his wit, marvelled at his cheerfulness in the face of suffering and impending death. One particular outburst used to send the young Doctor into spasms of laughter, namely, "Put out your tongue, Peter?" the old Fisherman would say mimicking the young Doctor, and then he would add: "My fee, Peter," and he would show how the young Doctor put out his hand for the money. This amused instead of angered the young Doctor, who knew the day was fast approaching when the old Fisherman would ask directly:

"Doctor, do I have cancer!"

The patient turned and sat on the edge of the bed and looked nostalgically out the Bay. "When will I be fit to pull an oar, Doctor?" he put in before answering the young Doctor's question. The young Doctor replied mysteriously as he shut the medical case. Another evasive answer maddened the old Fisherman.

"I'm not getting any better — worse if anything," he asserted in an accusing manner. "For eighteen months, Doctor, you have been attending this old Fisherman and damn the bit of you knows what is the matter with him beside the fact that he has pains in his guts and has to run every ten minutes to the toilet. And still, you can't tell him the name of his complaint. I'm afraid you know little or nothing about medicine; I'm afraid you're an ignorant man with a black bag full of instruments and pills —".

"I must know something about medicine," the young Doctor began to defend himself. "I attended Knockdun National School for eight, St. Eunan's College for five, and University College for six, years. Then I did my one year of Intern at St. Andrew's University Hospital; Gynaecology for one year at the University of Glasgow School of Midwifery; and Public Health at Trinity College for a year." The young Doctor listed other Institutions at which he had studied. "and now I have completed my third year as a General Practitioner, so I must know something about medicine, Peter?" He did not seem to be one bit annoyed at his knowledge being questioned by the old Fisherman, because he felt sorry for him and knew that, deep down, the patient trusted implicitly in his competence. If some one else had cast reflections upon his qualifications as a physician, the young Doctor would have been more than annoyed and demanded an apology.

The old Fisherman was impressed. He envied the young Doctor's learning as well as his health. Before he could reply the donkey began to roar: "E-aw, e-aw, e-aw, e-aw . . . ."

"There he goes again, Deeney's Jackass, roaring his big mouth off," said the old Fisherman impatiently. "I'm persecuted by that stupid and lazy swine."

The young Doctor smiled: "That donkey has good lungs."

He reached for his medical case with one hand and opened the door with the other. "So I must know something about medicine after all that schooling, Peter?"

The donkey had stopped roaring. "I'm glad that that racket is over," said the old Fisherman with a sigh of relief. Then he replied to the young Doctor's question: "Aye, you might impress the rest of your patients by listing off all those fancy schools you attended in your time. I must admit their renown is wide-spread, but, like all schools, they must have produced a few quacks too. Are you going to tell me the name of my complaint?"

The young Doctor hedged. "In a few weeks I should be in a position to give you a more informed opinion." With that he bade his patient good-bye.

"Hold on a minute, Doctor, not so fast," the old Fisherman demanded. "You won't tell me the name of my complaint because you don't know what's wrong with me. I say you are an ignorant man with a black bag."

The young Doctor smiled at this sally. "I'll see you again next week, D.V." he told the old Fisherman and he went out of the room. In frustration, the old Fisherman shouted after him:

"If Deeney's Jackass were studying at Oxford and Cambridge Universities for f-i-f-t-y y-e-a-r-s, he'd still know nothing about medicine!"

Soon the roar of the young Doctor's car came to the angry old Fisherman as the former sped towards Ards. "He didn't like the truth I told him," said the Fisherman to the walls, "so he is now taking his spite out on that old banger of a car he owns." Then he lay back exhausted and went asleep, Deeney's Donkey began to eat grass, and the curtains continued to sway in the window.

THE UNLUCKY TREE

The Fanad Peninsula actually extends from a line drawn from Bunlinn, Milford, to the Port Bridge, Letterkenny to the Atlantic Ocean. Some where north of this line there lived not so long ago three brothers whose names were Michael, James and Neil.

Michael was a farmer, James and Neil were carpenters, but all three were sometime fishermen. They worked together in an excellent spirit of co-operation. For example, Michael would help James and Neil to fell trees and draw them to the mill, and James and Neil would reciprocate, by helping Michael in the field and bog.

One day, the three brothers went to the wood to fell a pine tree. They were expert lumber-jacks and very careful workers. However, as the tree was about to fall, a gust of wind caused it to fall in a contrary direction, and the brothers barely managed to jump clear. Michael, who was older than James and Neil, was a bit slower; before he got quite away a branch ripped the buttons off his jacket. Slightly ruffled, the three brothers trimmed the branches and sawed the trunk into three parts of equal length.

Michael sliped the lengths through the wood with his horse, and carted them to James and Neil's sawmill. During the dangerous process of ripping the lengths into planks and boards, a plank fell from the bench and hurt Neil's foot. Fortunately, it was not very serious, and the pain went away after a few hours. Later, when James was planning and sawing the boards in the making of harrows, the saw slid off a knot and made a rather nasty cut in the index finger of his left hand. The wound, however, healed quickly with the aid of an anticeptic and a lint bandage.

Michael carted the harrows from the workshop to the beach where their boat was anchored, James and Neil put them on board, and the three brothers sailed across Lough Swilly to the market in Buncrana. They sold all but two of the harrows, and, as it was getting on in the day and looked like raining, they set out for home. When they were level with the Battery, a heavy shower began, the wind suddenly increased to the point where their little boat capsized, throwing them into the water.

The brothers' predicament was observed by another fisherman, who shouted the news to neighbours. His name was Big Eddy. He rallied four or five others in the launching of Big Dennis' boat, to the rescue. Although Big Dennis' boat was long and heavy and normally required the strength of ten men to move it, the five or six men managed to push it into the water without difficulty. Later, when they reviewed all aspects of the rescue, they regarded the ease with which they had launched Big Dennis' boat as nothing short of miraculous.

Meanwhile, the brothers themselves were hanging onto the keel of their boat. James, who thought he saw another boat coming to their aid, kept shouting encouragingly:

"There's a boat coming, men, hold on tight."

Michael and Neil prayed aloud for help to the Blessed Virgin. In the hilly village where their family lived, their women-folk, having seen their boat capsize and bearing in mind the fact that none of the brothers could swim, went down on their knees and recited the Rosary by way of intercession to Our Lady.

The water was cold. The brothers' hands rapidly grew numb. A large wave hit the boat, carrying Neil away with it. However, he managed to get back to the boat and resume his hold on the keel. Later, when he reviewed his experience, he was positive that he actually walked nine or ten steps upon the water in his effort to reach the boat. Neil, like his brothers, was a truthful man.

At last, Big Dennis' boat and its crew reached the capsized boat, the brothers were pulled to safety, and they all went to work putting the capsized boat back on to an even keel. But the harrows had vanished.

"Ah, goras, what odds about the harrows; it's good to be alive," James told his brothers when they regretfully reported the harrows missing. "Sure, it's better to lose our harrows than our lives. Thanks be to God and the Blessed Virgin for saving us from drowning." Michael and Neil readily agreed.

The brothers never saw the harrows again. All considered, the harrows were made from an unlucky tree.

THE YANK COMES HOME

The steam train rolled into Letterkenny station. In a horse drawn trap at the upper end of the station sat an impatient David MacBar from Fanad. His brother, Marcus, was returning for a long holiday after a lengthy exile in America. For weeks he had been looking forward to the Yank's homecoming. The last hour of waiting was the longest hour.

"I wonder will Marcus know me?" David mused. "Forty years is a long time; a man forgets. He is younger by two years but still I have changed a hell of a lot in all that time. I am sure he has changed. I wonder will I know him?"

Before David could put further questions to himself Marcus stepped off the train.

"That is Marcus now," David exclaimed with excitement; "I would know him a mile away on my father, God be good to him." David gave his horse a light whack of the rod. "Get up there, Bess; Marcus has a heap of trunks with him," David noted as he made his way forward.

Bess could not go any further without knocking visitors and friends to the ground so he jumped over the side of the trap. "Hold it Bess; Woo up there, Bess." The mare was quiet. He ran over to the only Yank to have come off the train. The Yank was pushing through the crowd when David caught him by the arm as he passed.

"Marcus," David greeted him loudly, "you stand the times rightly. How are you, Marcus?"

The Yank was dressed in a light grey suit; he wore an open-necked white shirt with its collar spread over the neck of his jacket; he wore white tennis shoes; and a pair of binoculars and a camera hung from his neck on straps of fine black leather. He also wore a white Texas hat and light rimmed glasses. David had seen photographs of the new President of the United States, Harry S. Truman, and could have sworn that Harry Truman and Marcus MacBar were sibb.

"Lord All-Mighty," Marcus exclaimed in his fully fledged Yanky accent, "it is my big, ugly brother, David MacBar. And how are you at all? I guess you are fine; sure you are fine; let me look at you." He pushed David back and looked him over critically.

David was the typical Fanadman of his day. He wore a navy blue suit, reddish brown shoes, red necktie, and a grey tweed cap. He considered himself well dressed on that day because during Fair Days he usually wore corduroy trousers, a second-hand jacket, polar-necked jersey, and a pair of boots. But he could see that Marcus disapproved.

"Gee, David, that dress went out thirty years ago in the States," Marcus said shaking his head. "I'll give you some of my duds. I brought you a brand new suit of light grey and a hat to match. For the love of Mike, get rid of that old-fashioned cap because it makes you look awfully foolish. Besides, you have grown very old." He looked about him.

David stood staring at his brother. Despite his brother harsh comments he felt tears flowing down his face with happiness at his brother's home-coming. "I am glad to see you again and safely home in Donegal after all those long years in America, Marcus. I'm glad you have come home at last. You should have come back twenty-five years ago. Come on, let me help you with the trunks?" David stooped to lift two trunks.

"They are not trunks, stupid," Marcus said as the two of them threw four large boxes by their handles into the back of the trap. "They are called cases. Will your nag be able to carry them and the two of us all the way to "Between-the-Waters" without lying down and dying?" He looked Bess over very critically. "Have you been feeding her good with oats? What have you been giving her — water? I guess what that nag needs is a good feed of oats. You always worked your nags too hard, David, and never gave them enough to eat with meanness — why, at home in Texas — I have a spread of some six and a half thousand acres of good land, we feed horses good; we give them plenty water and oats and their head; in this way we get things done and go places."

David felt that his brother had so changed over the last forty years, that he was a different person. He did not like his attitude or his words of complaint.

Bess moved out of the station in the direction of the Mountain Top. As they passed the general hospital, Marcus ran down clinics in Ireland; he criticised travel facilities, the rough conditions of the roads, and so on. When passing the mental hospital he talked strangely about the mental health of the Irish at home and abroad, saying:

"I guess the Irish are fools the world over through their drinking, their ignorance, and their superstition . . ."

David began to think Marcus could be doing with a few weeks inside. "He has changed for the worse," David said, coming to this regretful conclusion. "When he left Ireland he was the silent type, but now, God help us, no woman could hold to him for tempting chat." David recalled what Marcus had said to him at the station:

"You are still the same David, the same clothes, the same trap, the same horse — no, I guess not, horses don't live that long; the same station," and, looking about him with an air of sarcasm, Marcus continued; "Things have not changed one little bit. Gee, this country is still a rat hole. What have your politicians been doing all those forty years — fighting each other and hoodwinking the stupid Irish? No progress, David, no progress. You need the Democrats here. To the zoo with Republicans. They are for the big-shots, David. Ireland will not progress until it has a good Democratic Party in Power, why, in Texas, where I'm in the State Legislature, we would be cleaning up, building up, and shutting up the mugs who are keeping Ireland a John Bull's pig-house . . ."

Having gone beyond Ballyarr Marcus asked David how Mrs and the kids were living. "Ara begod, Vera, is fine, and so are the wanes. But we have no kids at all. I don't know if there is as much as one goat in the whole of Fanad," David said.

"O, David, you dumb brother," Marcus roared with laughter. "I guess you do not know that in the States we call children kids for short. Wanes, that is a rather quaint word. I guess we never hear it nowadays. Ireland has not changed one little bit since I left for America forty-two years, six months, and twenty days ago . . ."

They were now approaching Milford. Yet Marcus was talking almost continuously. David's head was aching from his criticism of the quality of crops, herds, and other aspects of farming and Irish life. In comparison to America, and all things American, everything in Ireland was a score of years behind in Marcus' estimation. Like a good Irishman, David did not like to listen to his country being run down in such a bitter way by anybody, his own brother not excepted. He felt like retaliating, but so far he had controlled his temper nicely, for how long he did not know.

"Your Mrs. wrote me that you built a new house with some of the many hundreds of dollars I sent home over the past forty-two years," Marcus remarked emphasising his contribution moneywise.

"I did indeed," David replied. "I got Shan MacGowan from Greeve to do the masonry and Hughie Doherty of Ucterlinn to do the carpentry. It's a fine house as you will see, with three rooms down stairs and three rooms up stairs —"

"Has it running water, central heating, and indoor toilets?" Marcus cut in to ask.

"What are indoor toilets?

"For the love of Mike, David, do you mean to say that you do not know what toilets are? Why that is absolutely pre-posterous," Marcus said in as fierce a tone as that of a madman, David thought.

"How in the name of St. Colmcille," David asked himself, "am I going to put up with this Yank's blowing and bumming while he is here on a holiday. Has he gone out of his latitude? One would think that since he left 'Between the Waters' that he would have learned to hold his tongue and not make an ediot of himself. If all Yanks are like Marcus, how the hell did they beat the Japs in the last war?

When they were passing the Workhouse David said through boredom, and to change the conversation for the umpteenth time: "That is the old Milford Workhouse, so it is."

"They possessed no sense of purpose then either," Marcus commented, "to have built a social service department in a bog. I guess they wanted the inmates, who were too damned lazy to work and look after themselves, to be punished with malaria. You know, I trust, what malaria is and where it is prevalent?" the Yank asked maliciously. "I guess, over here they are so grossly uneducated that I am heartily amazed how they can manage to survive. Sure, in the States, the standard of education in our primary schools is on par with Irish universities in the standard of learning. Sure they are or next door to it. I studied for a high school diploma while working in the mines, and thereafter, when I got enough dollars together, I studied full-time at the State university for a degree in engineering. But you, David, can you write a decent letter or read the newspaper intelligently?" Marcus spoke superciliously and David could not fail to be personally hurt because he had never got past the primary school level in education, his wife having to write his letters and read all but the simplest of newspaper articles and other such like material and government forms. It made him feel inadequate and stupid, and, as usually happens when a Donegalman's self-esteem gets a knock, he got as mad as hell and felt like striking out with either his fist or tongue or both together. But instead of striking out at Marcus David, disgusted with the attitude and language of his Yankee brother, resolved to let the Yank's words in one ear and out another and give him the full force of the 'silent treatment'. However, when they drew near to Milford Bakery, which was a building of considerable height and girth and situated on the bank of Mulroy Bay along the road leading from Milford and Kerrykeel, Marcus pointed and exclaimed with surprise:

"Look, David, see that there conglomerate? What is it, I guess?"

For a moment David did not bother to answer because he was afraid that what he might say by way of explanation would be turned against him by his sarcastic Yankee brother, and he felt Marcus had abused him enough with insults and mean gibes; but a bit of inspiration came to him which, if handled adroitly, could knock the conceit and braggartry out of the Yank. Turning slowly about, he asked casually:

"Which conglomerate?"

"I guess, to that there one," Marcus said. "What is it? I guess it was not there forty-two years ago when I went to the States!"

David smiled.

"Is it a factory or a block of flats?" Marcus speculated.

Recalling what the Yank had said about how big every thing was in the States — big houses, broad roads, and how fast the Yanks could build houses, roads, and so on, and disgusted at Marcus' outrageous bragging, David, inwardly gleeful for an opportunity to give the Yank a dig and a hint, spoke despite his resolve to be silent:

"I haven't got a clue, at all at all, for it wasn't there this morning when Bess and me were passing on our way to meet you at the Lough Swilly Railway station in Letterkenny!"

When the Yank spoke again several minutes later every thing big-big about America seemed to have gone entirely out of his head.

THE CRESSLOUGH FAIR

My cousin Charley lived in Drumcreeve. He was a farmer, who owned one old cow. This old cow was losing her teeth and failing in milk.

It was the month of December. The days were dark, short and cold, while the nights were long, lonesome and dark — very dark. A light covering of snow lay on the ground and the women and children of Drumcreeve were preparing for the Holy season of Christmas.

One evening, when Charley was sitting down to a supper of milk and porridge, his wife came in from the byre.

"Go easy with the milk, dear," she prudently advised Charley when she saw him with a large bowl of milk in front of him. "Look at how little milk Betty gave me today!" She put a bucket on the table for her husband's inspection; then she sighed despondently.

Poor Charley felt guilty. Here he was, the head of the household, sitting down to drink a full bowlful of milk, and children in the house in need of it.

"I am weaning the baby because I, too, am failing in milk; if I allow Teresa to go on sucking until she is 12 months old, I will be skin and bones — and perhaps a *bedrill*! Something has got to be done at once, dear?"

"Of course! What do you suggest, love?" My cousin was a polite, refined man.

"Och, what do I know, dear. Buy another cow, I suppose?"

"That is what I will do, love, at the next opportunity!"

"Sooner than that!" She was adamant.

The poor man was thinking: '£3 for a cow in the Fair of

Milford, £2 for a cow in Creeslough. I will have to travel to Creeslough Fair because I can only afford to part with £2!'

That was all the money he had in his possession. But the village of Creeslough was twice as far from his home as Milford, and what he would save in money he would have to spent travelling time. He made up his mind to go to the Fair of Creeslough and buy a cow.

"Thank you dear, you are very kind," Charley's wife said when he promised to bring home a springing cow from Creeslough the following fair-day. And she gave him a hug and a kiss.

One morning, about a week later, Charley got up early; it was still dark. He took his breakfast and set out for the fair with a blackthorn stick in his hand for protection and support, £2 in his trouser pocket, and the pipe in his mouth.

The sky was heavy. The snow had melted during the night but there was still a biting frost in the air. Charley was forced to pull the collar of his heavy army coat up round his ears and rub his hands occasionally.

Wearing a pair of hobnailed boots, Charley walked past the sleeping village of Milford, past the stirring village of Termon, down the long, lonesome road that runs from Termon to Creeslough, through the 'Gap of Barnes Beg'. He knew the road because he had often travelled that way when he was a young man dealing in sheep. He was by now growing tired and hungry; but, above all, he wanted to have another draw on the pipe. He had accidently left his spare box of matches behind him when he was leaving home and the distance of a few miles would have to be crossed before he would come to the nearest house. Being young and active he decided to take a short-cut through the moors, so that he could shorten the journey by more than a mile and arrive in the Fair before the cattlemen, for, by doing so, he would have his pick of the best cows, and he would get a light for his pipe that much sooner; he cut through the moors at the Bear's Head.

When he was young, going on pilgrimages to Doonwell, he thought he saw a group of big rocks the very image of a bear's head in those moors. And they reminded him of the map of Donegal, which looks like a bear's head in profile.

Long ago there were giants living in Donegal, and they

used to play games with rocks — making designs, building castles, throwing rocks at each other from the tops of hills.

Charley crossed the moors not far from these rocks. The morning was still quite dark on the moors, but he knew the way; he stumbled onto an old mountain track running across the moors over which he had often travelled when he was buying or selling sheep.

Suddenly Charley saw a light in the distance. "A house," he says to himself. "I did not know any one lived on the moors?"

Charley tried to recall having seen a house there. "No house? Maybe some one has been evicted from his home in Creeslough for non-payment of rent and has come out here to build a rough shanty of turf, fir, and rushes to protect himself, and his family, from the elements!"

How and ever, Charley walked on and thought: 'I will knock on his door and ask for a light for my pipe'.

And so he went over to the door. It was one of those old-style half-doors; he knocked sharply. Then he looked over the door: An old man and an old woman were sitting smoking pipes by the fire, and Charley entered without hesitation.

"I am very sorry for the intrusion at this unreasonable hour of the morning; I saw your light and thought I would impose upon your kindness and hospitality; I am looking for a light for my pipe."

The old man got up and shook Charley's hand vigorously, and said:

"Musha! How are you, Charley O'Doherty?" Then he walked past Charley and out the door.

The old woman stood up, smiled, and greeted Charley maternally.

"Musha! How are you doing, Charley O'Doherty?" And she, too, walked outside.

Thinking that they had gone outside for turf to put on the fire, Charley waited for the old couple to return after he had lit his pipe. He looked about the room as a man is wont to do; he noted that it was a single-end, with no rooms leading off from the living-room. He thought it odd that there were no holy pictures hanging on the walls; the furniture, vessels, and decorations seemed foreign — and, coming to think of it,

Charley considered the old couple rather dwarfish and peculiar looking, and strangely dressed . . . suddenly he felt
frightened!

"Is this a kind of trap I am in?"

In olden times cattle-dealers were often robbed of their
money and finally murdered.

"Maybe they take me for a cattleman and are planning to
rob and kill me!"

A voice inside his head seemed to be saying: 'Get out of
this house before the old man and old woman return!"

Charley was pale with fright. He went out the door quickly
and walked briskly for a hundred yards before slackening his
pace and loosening his grip on his blackthorn stick He looked behind him, to see if he were being followed . . .

The light had gone out. Dawn was coming up. But Charley
could not, however, see the house. All he could see was a big
rock! And this particular rock stands in the same relationship
to the group of rocks — called the Bear's Head — as the Island
of Aranmore stands to the Mainland of Donegal. Charley
thought the whole episode very odd.

My cousin Charley was a wise, sober, and truthful man. He
told me he saw the faeries in a rock near the Bear's Head.
That was his fixed opinion.

I am inclined to believe him.

REFLECTIONS ON THE LAKE OF SHADOWS

I woke up from a sound sleep and looked out the window of my bedroom at a beautiful July morning.

"Barney is getting a splendid day for making hay," I said to myself.

Willie, his son, had called to see me the previous night to ask for my help in the hay-field. I told him: "I will be delighted to give you a hand to tie hay tomorrow — if I am alive and well."

I got dressed quickly, eat my breakfast hurriedly, and set out for work in Newbridge, enthusiastically.

The first person I met on my arrival at Barney's home, was his wife.

"Good morning. Come in, and have some tea before you, and the other men, go to the fields," she said, pleasantly, and smiled.

"I do not mind if I do," I said and followed her inside her neatly kept house. Barney was sitting up in bed smoking and looking the picture of contentment.

"Top o' the morning to you, Dano," says he good humouredly, in greeting.

"The top and the bottom o' the morning to you, too, Barney," I replied rather brazenly. I knew he would not pass any heed on my high spirits. He was that kind of person.

Minutes later Ambrose came into the room and bid us all 'time o' day'. He, too, had come with much good cheer and goodwill to give Barney a help with the hay.

Barney's wife made tea, and, while we drank it leisurely, Barney puffed his cigarette and told one story after another.

When starting time arrived, I reluctantly followed the others out to the hay-field, because I would have liked to listen for hours to the stories Barney loved telling. Another time, perhaps, I thought hopefully.

Apart from being a first-rate storyteller, Barney had many other excellent qualities and had worked at many trades during his long, eventful life: labourer in Scotland, merchant, farmer, salesman and sometime fisherman. But above all else he was a fisherman. He really loved the sea. He had been a good and skilled fisherman in his prime, I heard his neighbours say.

A violent storm a few years back had sent him into retirement, prematurely. The breakwater was inadequate to prevent his trawler from being smashed to pieces upon the rocks by the giant waves and gale-force winds of an Irish winter. It was heartbreaking to see the wreckage of his treasured trawler scattered, forlornly, in the small harbour — after the abation of the storm; and to think that his principal means of earning a livelihood was gone, for a time at least, or forever. To really appreciate fully the magnitude of such a loss, one must have the blood of fishermen in his veins or be a seaman of long standing.

When at primary school I used to see Barney's little grey trawler out fishing in the Swilly. How I longed to be a fisherman, too. I remember saying to other pupils:

"Barney is having a grand day for the fishing."

They would reply understandingly:

"He is surely. Wouldn't it be nice out there beside him, trawling?"

I suppose we all dreamed about being fishermen some day, owning our own boats and equipment, and fishing in our own, dear Swilly. To school-children like ourselves, Barney's boat was an essential part of our lives because we daydreamed, and his trawler, like the Buncrana train, was a landmark we saw no more after the storm. We were, I recall, emotionally upset by this minor, but very real sea disaster.

When adverse circumstances forced Barney to give up fishing, he took up farming with equal devotion. His farm was small but he augmented his yields by renting land from neighbours who were not cultivating their land.

On the day in question we went to work in a large field with a heavy crop. Barney paid us a visit shortly before lunchtime, to chat and see how work was progressing. I listened to him while he described, vividly, several of his exploits during his days in Scotland as a young man. They were fascinating.

He visited us again in the afternoon, bringing tea and sandwiches, by which time we were much advanced with our work, and he was childishly pleased.

All hands sat down in the hay-field to eat and drink and while we were thus engaged, a small sailing-boat went by in the lough below. The white sails in the blue Swilly, green fields and purple hills on both banks of the inlet, with a blue sky and a few white cloudlets overhead, made a truly picturesque sight. We talked about fishing, sailing, and a hundred and one other things connected with the sea, and sea-faring generally. At that time, and in that place, we considered the Swilly to be the most beautiful place on earth!

We discussed at length and in awe the tragic death of Jim Brown and his brother, Bertie. They were fishermen too. They had been salmon fishing when their boat, the Abbeyfoyle, either floundered in a gale, or foundered upon the rocks, the previous month. Because we knew the Brown brothers personally, we were sad beyond mention. We were also sad about the death of young Porter, from Burt, and old Carter, from Fahan; they were members of the crew of the Abbeyfoyle when it sank.

Lough Swilly has claimed the lives of many good fishermen — including the life of my close and youthful acquaintance, Alphonsus MacGill, of St. Johnson, but I do not think we shall ever forget the Abbeyfoyle disaster.

"The Swilly will never be the same without Jim and Bertie Brown," said I gravely to no one in particular. I was on the brink of tears!

"True Dano!" Barney confirmed, solemnly. "They were expert seamen and good fishermen . . . and very obliging . . ." He looked about him, sadly.

"Perhaps," I said mentally, "he is thinking, what I have been thinking for weeks past, that the Abbeyfoyle, and its owners, is another landmark we will never see again; no more would we be crossing the Swilly in the Abbeyfoyle to watch soccer finals in Buncrana.

"At one time," Barney said historically, "the Swilly was a busy waterway, with fishing fleets, battle fleets, crafts and boats of many designs and sizes. Today, look at it: nothing really — little traffic: more aeroplanes fly over our heads than ships and boats go up and down that Lough. This is most regrettable! The Swilly ought to be busy as the Thames, or the Mersey, or the Clyde. Flag-waving is all very fine, patriotic and exciting, but, the getting back of the ports, in 1939, into our own hands, did not help the Swilly much."

We looked down on the Swilly and thought about the strange twists of politics and economics, and we were dreaming again.

After we returned to our work, Barney dodged homewards, slowly. We did a good job and had the hay tied, and finished off, by mid-evening; then we, too, dodged slowly towards Barney's residence, for tea, and wages.

After we had drank the tea, Ambrose and I moved outside to the cool air; Barney, who was already sitting in the shade, took out his wallet and asked us to mention the 'damage'. We told him the wages we wanted and he paid us willingly. Then he started storytelling once more.

Ambrose and I sat down on lobster-pots and made ourselves comfortable. Barney, who was sitting on an upturned little boat, lit a cigarette and Ambrose filled his pipe and I nibbled on a piece of toffee.

Barney told many stories but one story in particular brought out, very vividly, I thought, the fact that courts of law do recognise and indeed exercise class distinction.

"There is the tale told of two tramps," Barney began, "who lived in tents by the wayside. They were the proud owners of two sturdy horses. Because they did not have land of their own, on which to graze their horses, they grazed them on the grass growing along the public road.

"This went on for years, but one day the local Sergeant of the Gardai caught these tramps grazing their horses in this fashion and pinned a summons to the District Court on our two friends.

"On the day of the hearing, they appeared in court in good

time and dress. The Judge asked the first tramp his name and occupation. 'My name is MacGinley, I'm a tinker, your Honour'. 'And pray tell us, what is your address, my good man?'. 'No fixed abode, your Honour, sir', MacGinley replied, politely. 'For grazing your horse along the public highway and liable, therefore, to cause an obstruction, I hereby fine you £2'.

"The second tramp was called next. 'What is your name and occupation, my good man?' the Judge enquired. 'I'm O'Doherty, sir; I'm a tinker, too, your Honour', the second tramp replied fervently. 'What is your address?' the Judge asked courteously. 'I've a room taken off Mr. MacGinley, here, sir, your Honour'. The Judge looked him over closely and then looked at Mr. MacGinley, and said:

" 'I hereby fine you £1, Mr. O'Doherty'!"

We saw the inference and admitted, on the spot, that O'Doherty was quite a clever fellow for having played on the Judge's social susceptibilities."

"That reminds me," I said, "of a fellow, who lived in the Buncrana District, by the name of Leo Tolstoy MacLoughlin. He owned a very small farm, and times were hard with him and his charming wife, Jane. The Parish Priest of Cockhill advertised for a sexton, the salary for the year being £10. The vacancy was convenient for our friend, so his wife advised him to put an application in for the position.

"The Priest says, 'MacLoughlin, you are the very man I want for the job; you live nearby and ought to have no bother slipping over here to the chapel to ring the bell at nine o'clock in the morning, at 12 o'clock noon, and at six o'clock in the evening. Please sign this form . . . a contract for the coming year; just a formality.'

"MacLoughlin's heart sank low in his stout breast. 'Acha! — Father, I'm very sorry to have troubled you; sure I can't sign my name'.

" 'Well, in that case', the Priest explained in an understanding manner, 'I am very, very sorry — I cannot give you the job, because, you see there would be the occasional note to be read, and so on; but no harm done, my son.'

" 'I quite understand, Father'!"

"MacLoughlin went home to his wife a very disappointed

man because he was not educated and had failed to get the job on that score. The vacancy, he knew, was opportune and he had really set his heart on supplementing his meagre income by £10. 'If only I had an education like other people I know', he told his wife sadly, 'I would've been signed on, there and then'. He felt rejected and he cursed his tough luck. Then, as time passed, he forgot the affair, and some months later he started taking the odd load of turf to Derry City to sell to various house-wives in the Strand Road area.

"After being a year in business, he put two extra carts on the road; the following year he had a sizeable fleet of carts on the road; and, after seven, or eight years in business, he not alone had had a large fleet of carts on the road, but he also owned a shop in that city, and had three Ford lorries on hire to respectable contractors engaged in general road-haulage and the mountain transportation service. He was in business barely ten years when he was running five shops in Derry, owned a fleet of lorries, had a substantial holding and interest in other commercial undertakings, and was director of a number of private companies operating in the field of civil-engineering, banking, insurance, entertainment, and so on.

"Then, one day, he goes into his bank in Buncrana in order to sign some important document. Of late, this bank had come under new management and the official dealing with MacLoughlin's account was not familiar with his client's background and personal attributes. The official had been briefed on MacLoughlin's personal standing, business history, and business involvement — therefore he knew quite a bit about his client's property, business success and relevant data . . But he did not know his client was illiterate.

"During their meeting, which took place in the manager's spacious office, at the back-wing of the three-storey building on the southside of Atlantic Avenue, the official, Emmet MacTone, pushed an important document across the desk towards Mr. MacLoughlin, and said:
" 'Mr. MacLoughlin, please sign your name on the dotted line'."

"Mr. MacTone was surprised when the document was pushed back, marked with an X where MacLoughlin's signature ought to have been written.

" 'What's the meaning of this?' the official said, When he saw the X. 'Are you, by any chance, playing a joke on the new manager, Mr. MacLoughlin?'

" 'No indeed, I'm not; I'm far too busy to have time for jokes. I have no education – I can't sign my name'!

" 'You tell me you cannot sign your name and yet you made all this money in business?' The Manager said, looking closely at the bank's wealthiest client to see if he could detact any trace of a suppressed smile on his lips or humour in his eyes.

"The Manager could see MacLoughlin was in earnest, that he could not sign his name. Baffled he asked:

" 'Mr. MacLoughlin, you say you have no education, that you are illiterate, not able to sign your name? What? And yet you made all this . . . eh . . . money in business . . .?"

" 'I did indeed', MacLoughlin said modestly.

Still looking baffled, the Manager speculated:

" 'What would you be doing now, if you had received, say, as good an education as mine?'

"MacLoughlin replied with a smile: 'I would be up there in Cockhill ringing the Parish bell for £10 or £20 a year!' "

We laughed. Barney and Ambrose marvelled at this unusual social phenomenon. Ambrose took a long puff of his pipe and spat on the ground and not to be outdone, began:

"Mulrine (Ambrose's maternal grand-uncle) was having a lint-pulling party. We were sitting at the dinner table. Mulrine sat at the head of the table; Edward Deeney – Mulrine's cousin, Tommy William and Johnny Burke sat on his left; Tommy Eddie (the writer's maternal uncle), Pat Gallagher and my brother James sat on his right; and I myself sat at the bottom of the table.

"About half-way through dinner Tommy Eddie was telling a story of an Englishman, known locally as John MacCormack-Smith, of the labouring class, who emigrated to New York.

" 'When Smith went on board his ship at Liverpool, there wasn't a soul to see him off and help him along on board. In America, he got a job in a stone-quarry, and while working he had a habit of singing all kinds of songs to amuse himself.

" 'One day a travelling surveyor, who was interested in music, heard Smith sing and liked his voice. He knew it was a unique voice — the kind of voice the public would go for in a big way. So, the surveyor asked the Englishman if he would care to have his voice trained. Sure the young man thought the surveyor was joking, that he wanted him to stop singing and annoying the foreman and the other navvies. But, when the surveyor insisted and showed signs of being in earnest, Smith thought he would give it a try, if for no other reason than pleasing the whims of the surveyor, who was a very influential member of the firm.

" 'In no time at all Smith was singing in local halls, at concerts, dances, and the like. A big film company signed him on and within the space of a half a dozen years he was world famous and a millionaire into the bargain.

"And so, after an absence of ten years, John MacCormack-Smith decided to go back to England to see his own mother and father, and to have some peace and quiet. He returned on the same ship that had taken him to America — all for sentimental reasons. Although he had tried to keep his visit secret, word of it came to the attention of British newspapers and the docks at Liverpool were packed with reporters, dukes, politicians, and big shots of every description — all waiting to welcome him home to England and have the honour of making his acquaintance.

"As the ship was docking, Smith arrived on deck, and, after he had made some castic remarks about the other passengers, he was informed of the presence, at the docks, of a special reception-committee and of groups of big-shots who were so anxious to shake his hand and have the privilege of inviting him to their homes.

"Smith was silent for a moment, reflected, and exclaimed angrily:

" 'The dirty swine! The day I left England, a poor boy, there was no one to see me off; but now, when I'm rich and famous, every bloody scoundrel in England wants to lay his dirty hands on me. I'll tell you bastards what I'll do: I'll ignore you all — that's what I'll do, ignore the whole bloody lot of you!' Sticking his hands in his pockets, Smith walked off the ship, looking neither to the left or the right, and made a bee-line for a waiting taxi; he pulled his hat down on his eyes, took his hands out of his pockets, and ran to the taxi;

he was driven away to his parental home in Sheffield — leaving the whole rickmatick standing flabbergasted on the quayside!' "

" 'He ought to have exercised discretion and showed good manners by passing himself off notwithstanding his contempt for the big-shots; he showed his bad breeding by adopting that attitude', Edward Deeney said, academically.

" 'I agree with you, Edward', Tommy William said in a superior manner. 'Smith should have passed himself off, as you say, as pleasantly as he knew how no matter how he felt inside.'

"The other men made various comments along the same lines, but Mulrine said nothing as if he wasn't listening. Being an ambitious man, with no sympathy at all for the aristocracy, hating snobbery, he appreciated the feelings of Smith, who had had to struggle hard in a foreign land for fame and fortune with little or no help from big-shots in England.

"Mulrine was lifting a flowery potato in his fork when his patience gave out, and, growing very flushed, he could not contain his temper any longer;

" 'Well, upon my sock,' Mulrine shouted passionately, 'Smith, was a man after my own heart, for he did what I would have done myself if I were in his position;' and, bringing his fist down violently on the table, he sent the flowery potato flying in a thousand pieces along the entire length of the table. 'Smith did exactly what I would have done myself! Big-shots my arse!'

" 'Decorum at the dinner table, please, gentlemen,' Edward Deeney expostulated, looking indignantly at Mulrine. Edward was cultured, well-read, and docile.

" 'James, fearing that a punch-up might commence if feelings were allowed to run much higher, deliberately switched the conversation to a discussion of beautiful women; and calm and decorum and merriment returned once more to Mulrine's dinner table!' "

I longed to tell more stories, and to listen to more stories being told by my two associates, but Ambrose was impatient to get home, because, he said, he had chores to do; since he lived on a farm in my own townland, and would be travelling homewards by my road, I, too, bid good evening to Barney and set out for home, accompanied by Ambrose.

The sun was just setting when I arrived at home. Not wanting to go to bed while it was still day-light, I decided to pay a visit to my cousin, John Banker-Doherty.

John was a musician who often gave me hair-cuts.

After John had cut my hair, he played tunes on the accordion; his mother made tea; his sister showed me her school-books, his grandmother told me tales of long ago; then I returned home – tired but happy!

It had been a beautiful day!

BURIAL IN CALIFORNIA

James was exhausted by the time he reached the summit of the Carradoan Hills on that hot afternoon. It was late summer. And, for any man of seventy years, even though he be in good health, the climb was a rather difficult task.

The space of almost half a century had gone by since the day he had last climbed these hills and sat on the blue-whinstone rock, which crowned the summit. He remembered it was a Sunday evening. In those days it was the fashion to climb these hills at least once in a lifetime and sit on this rock, which was known locally as "Clogh-na-Scamaill".

James' sisters and brothers had sat on this rock before their going across the sea, and many bitter tears were shed on it in times gone by.

James did not know for certain what impelling force had caused him to make the ascent, on foot, on such a warm day, in his old age; however, he was positive – as he filled and smoked his American pipe in the peace and quietude of the summit, and looked down from his vantage point at the valley – that there existed some vital connection between those two points in time. Perhaps, he figured, it was an unconscious desire for a spiritual stock-taking exercise – a preparation for his inevitable journey to the 'America of Eternity'?. Whatever force it was, he knew he would not hesitate to meet and converse with it, and to find peace of soul and come to terms with life, and impending death!

A strong, cool, refreshing breeze blew across the summit, shaking the purple-blossomed heather and making soft rustling sounds among the rocks and ridges of the hills. The rock was the ideal spot, he knew, for transcendental meditation and reminiscing.

Because there was no haze he could see Burt, Inch, Inishowen, Dun Ri, Drumhalla, Ucterlinn, and the Church of St. Catherine of Siena – perfectly – well, almost perfectly; over the years his eyes had grown a little weak; they tired and watered easily from the strain of concentrated gazing in sunshine or snow. He regretted not having taken along his telescope, for he would have liked very much to have observed farmers working in their fields and fishermen trawling in Lough Swilly. Yet, he recalled that, on setting out from his nephew's house in Upper Clondallon, he did not have any notion whatsoever of ascending the Carradoan Hills. The urge to do so came to him suddenly while he was strolling casually through the fields of his nephew's farm which were adjacent to the foot of the hills.

When he compared today's view of the valley with that of forty years before, he saw little change. True, a few new homesteads (as he called them affectionately) had been erected, whilst others had fallen into various stages of decay, and smoke no longer emanated from their chimneys; but such changes were, he knew, to be expected in fifty or even forty years. The landscape had changed, somewhat: Many trees and bushes, he observed, had sprung up, and a greater number of fields lay uncultivated. Hay had become – obviously – a popular crop, he noted with interest. The landscape showed many shades of green because of the large range and variety of crops; and, altogether, the countryside looked more prosperous. He attributed this fact to improved farming methods, artificial fertilisers and a gradual but general increase in prosperity and education.

As James sat smoking and inhaling the invigorating air of

the summit, he cast his mind back to the day, forty years ago, he had last sat on Clogh-na-Scamaill. He was then in his early twenties and had just returned home from Scotland, where he had been working at the docks in Glasgow. That day, of long ago, he had climbed the Carradoan Hills to have a 'farewell look' at the valley and the Lake of Shadows before going to America.

America held attractive prospects for him at the time, so he went there. Although good fortune was slow in visiting him, America proved, in the long run, to be a kind country to him. He worked in several industrial cities of the East, on cattle ranches in the Mid-West — from Texas to Nebraska, fought all through the four years of Civil War in the famous '69th' (an Irish Regiment in the Union Army), and ended up owning gold, silver and copper mines in California.

James had once told a friend: "I fought for Uncle Sam, but he paid me good."

James was wont to admit that all the beauty he had seen in Scotland, Ireland, and America was ordinary when compared with the glittering panorama of Lough Swilly and its surrounding districts.

"No wonder," he said mentally, "I came back to die in Donegal, and to be buried in Killygarvan graveyard with my parents, sisters and my immediate ancestors . . ."

Yet he had had a lonely feeling that destiny willed otherwise. Facts were there to support it.

On his arrival in Drumhalla after a long absence from home — in which no correspondence worth mentioning had passed in either direction — he found his parents dead and their house and farm owned by a next-door neighbour. It transpired that a younger brother, unable to support his wife and large family on their home farm in Cnocdubh, sold out and went to live in Scotland — settling finally in Glasgow.

James' plans were, therefore, upset momentarily and for a time he took up residence with a nephew called Edward; but it proved to be of a temporary nature only because Edward, and his wife, had a large family, and were unable, or unwilling, to provide him with sufficient accommodation to meet his requirements and previous standards.

After leaving Edward and his wife, James moved into the

home of another nephew called Billy. Billy was a bachelor, who lived nearby, with a younger sister keeping house. After a few months in residence with Billy and his sister, James, generously offered to build a modern and spacious house for them.

"Billy, order the materials and hire the builders; I guess I will foot the bill," James told Billy one morning during breakfast.

That day Billy was in good humour and was delighted with this idea and readily accepted his uncle's generosity, because he knew the girls would be more susceptible to his romantic advances — they would simply love to live in such stately mansions as Yanks built! Some weeks later, before the project materialised, Billy rejected his uncle's offer; and this is why he did so.

Unfortunately Billy possessed two things he could very well have done without — namely, a mercurial temperament and a crowd of jealous and insincere advisers. He was hypersensitive to adverse criticism and public opinion, and, when excited, or vexed, always acted irrationally.

When he told these untrustworthy and unscrupulous advisers (Billy could not keep a secret of this kind) about his uncle's offer, being alarmed and envious, they retorted:

"Billy, how do you think your Uncle James made his money? The honest way? — no bloody fear! He has lived it rough out there with the cowboys and gold-diggers. When he builds the new house on your land, he will have you evicted, or something to that effect. Sure that caper is as old as the Hills of Ucterlinn . . ."

Billy was shocked and infuriated to think his own flesh and blood would entertain such a crooked idea — tricking him out of his inheritance. And so, he exploded, and told his advisers passionately:

"I do not care who he is, he will do no such thing — the dirty Yank; for I will not let him! . . ."

That night, Billy went home, raging, and gave his uncle his 'walking papers.'

"Get out of my house to hell," he told James in a gruff voice, without explanation. "You will not do me out of my farm! . . ."

Billy would have done James an injury if his sister had not restrained him and told him not to dare hit an old man who was also his uncle and guest.

James thought Billy was drunk or had gone crazy, but, when he was certain that neither of these conditions was present, he made a spirited reply:

"I do not know what you are talking about, Billy. I am your late mother's brother and you are my blood-nephew; I have done you no wrong nor do I intend doing you one, I guess. But, I guess, if you wish me to go — quit your homestead, I will return to America and be buried in California. I am too wealthy a man, besides, to have designs of any kind on your tiny and barren spread. But one thing I will tell you partner, because of your attitude you will not get one cent of my money when I pass out of this world."

Looking back on this stormy confrontation with Billy the previous night, in which he mentioned his intention of returning to California, James was sure that, at that time, he did not entertain any serious notion of returning to America: it was the only credible answer he could think of making at the time to Billy's unexpected and violent order to quit his domain. Now he knew he was returning to America: what future did he have in Ireland separated from the company of his nephews and nieces? Yet, to be buried in Killygarvan was a life-long dream and prayer.

By the time James set out on his descent the day was almost spent; evening had arrived, and he was worried that, if he were unduly late in returning, Billy's sister would be very concerned. James wanted to spare her unnecessary solicitude. She was really kind hearted, good natured, and sensible; he could not forget how quickly and courageously she had come to his assistance — she had protested to her brother against his harsh words to his uncle, but he knew Billy was a great fool and possibly mentally unbalanced. "Life is hard for her," James thought sorrowfully; "she has to work hard cleaning, cooking, sewing and slaving for her uncouth, ignorant and silly brother . . ."

For a moment James was aware of a strong temptation to remain all night on the summit, or, at least longer that evening, because of the glorious, serene, and peaceful atmosphere which reigned there; and he could not quite understand why he had not climbed the hills the day after his return from America.

At the beginning of the descent he studied, carefully, the geographical outline of Cnocdubh in the distance. Seeing this area, from an elevated and distant position, on a beautiful day, in early harvest, with the sun sinking behind Knockalla and throwing its rays across the sky and shadows across the valley and Lough, begot in his mind a feeling of nostalgia; and a multitude of pleasant memories came flooding through his mind's eye. Then, they were followed by unpleasant thoughts, which tortured his peace of mind: his parents and sisters were dead, his brothers were in exile; the older generations — his generations — were dead, and younger generations were growing up, or had grown up; his home no longer existed as such, and he was feeling like a virtual stranger in his own fatherland. There was a gap, he saw, of over forty years in his life — with respect to life in Ireland, a gap which could never be filled — no matter what he did now, he had left many important affairs too late for rectification.

"If only I had written home," he said, speaking to the hills around him, "I would have been in touch, things would not now seem so remote and strange; I should have been in touch — yet, I had very primitive education. I guess I should never have emigrated, leaving my parents and sisters and brothers, to follow a dream; I guess that is all it was? But I did become rich; but poor in friends. Such is life, I guess, my destiny . . ."

James was not interested in literature — poetry, prose, history, or any thing of that brand, but he could appreciate — at that moment — the personal loneliness and traumatic experience of Oisin on his return from Tir-na-nOg to find Finn and the Fianna dead for hundreds of years; or, the wonder and disturbing thoughts of the French Emigres returning to their country, in the train of Louis XVIII — following the defeat of Napoleon, after an exile of a quarter of a century; or, the bewilderment of Rip Van Winkle, returning home, after a sleep of twenty years in the Kaatskill Mountains, to discover his wife and children missing and his village inhabited by strangers, who did not know him!

Tired but contented James arrived back at his abode,

knowing for certain why he had climbed the Carradoan Hills a second time in his life: he was having another 'farewell look' at the valley and the Lake of Shadows.

Billy and his sister met James outside their dwelling-house, near the main gate.

"Where on earth have you been, Uncle James?" his niece said, obviously relieved and glad to see him. "You are late for dinner, and we were getting worried about you, but now we are delighted to see you are still with us and in good health . . ."

"I was up on the summit, sweetheart, honey," James replied gaily. "I guess it was glorious up there, you see."

Billy and his sister looked questioningly at each other, at the summit, and at their uncle, but said nothing.

The following morning James went into the nearest town and booked a passage to America; and in less than six weeks, with stoic resignation and fortitude, he sailed away, unobtrusively, from his native land, forever!

SWIMMING IN DEEP WATER

One very hot Sunday afternoon many years ago two brothers took their weekly swim in Donegal Bay. They were strong swimmers, that is to say, they could swim out to island rocks and swim safely back again. Swimming in deep water may have made them a little anxious but it did not frighten them. But to those who could swim only short distances it was safer to swim in shallow water and parallel with the shore.

When the brothers, who were named Charley and Eddy, had stopped swimming and had climbed ashore on a flat rock and had dried themselves well and had re-dressed, they lay down on a grassy slope for a smoke and a bit of relaxation after a week of hard work fishing and farming. Their collie dog, Prince, lay beside them. He would run about now and then chasing flies.

The brothers were some time enjoying a quiet chat and the view, and watching holiday-makers and locals swimming on beaches near by, when a man, whom they knew quite well, from the hill district, came by to have a dip in the Atlantic.

"Good day, Gallagher," the brothers said in greeting.

"A fine afternoon, thank God, boys," Gallagher said returning their greeting. He went beyond the brothers to the edge of the rock and began to undress.

"The water is nice and warm today, Gallagher," the brother named Charley said for the sake of conversation and to confirm Gallagher in his resolve to have a swim.

"Good, good," Gallagher said in acknowledgement as he discarded one garment after another. "Fine, fine, boys."

"It's about twenty feet deep at that point, Gallagher," the brother named Eddy warned him. "I suppose you are a good swimmer?"

"Nay, boys, I cannot swim a stroke, but, sure as everybody knows, if you go into deep enough water, you are bound to swim because the water is so strong there that it can float a ship like the Queen Mary. Who the hell can swim in shallow water?" Gallagher replied casting off his boots.

The brothers thought he was joking, for no one in his right mind and who could not swim strongly would venture into the water at that deep point where Gallagher was stripping off for a dip. Before another word of conversation passed between the three Donegalmen, Gallagher dived into Donegal Bay.

It is quite natural for those on the shore to watch those who are in bathing, swimming and diving or trying to do one or the other. Besides, as every Donegal fisherman knows, anyone, no matter how good a swimmer, can get into difficulties; a cramp, or swimming too quickly after a heavy meal, can prove fatal even to the best of swimmers. So the brothers kept a close watch on Gallagher's antics in the water.

They suddenly noticed that Gallagher surfaced struggling and then sank again. When he next surfaced he was really battling wildly like a fish on the hook. He choked and grasped about him in a frantic manner.

Prince began to bark.

The brothers realised at this stage that Gallagher had not been joking about not being able to swim and that he was in serious trouble. They jumped to their feet and ran to his assistance. The dog, too, ran to the edge of the rock, as if he, too, wanted to help Gallagher save himself from drowning.

Charley threw off his cap, coat, and boots; whilst Eddy, intending to help from the bank, unknotted their neckties and tied them together to form a rope.

Charley dived in and surfaced beyond Gallagher, who, like all drowning men, was reaching out to catch anything, or anybody, in order to keep afloat. Charley swam towards him. Gallagher was of middle age and of stocky build. To let him get a grip of a rescuer could be fatal for both of them. Charley came behind him and struck him a mighty blow on the side of the chin in order to render him unconscious for a few seconds; he turned Gallagher on his back, put his left hand under his chin, and swam using the right hand. Gallagher was just coming to his senses again when Eddy reached the rope to Charley, who pulled Gallagher and himself to safety with a little lift from Eddy.

When all were out of the water Charley took off his shirt, socks, trousers and underwear and spread them out to dry, whilst Eddy helped Gallagher to dry and dress himself. No talk passed between the three men; and, what usually happens on scattered Donegal beaches, none of the bathers, despite the barking of Prince, had come to Gallagher's rescue, perhaps none of them was aware that a man had nearly drowned that day in that part of Donegal Bay. If it had not been for the brothers, Gallagher would have drowned without anyone being aware of it.

Eventually Eddy said: "Gallagher, that was a close call? Never venture into deep water again until you have learned to swim in shallow water.

Charley, who had stretched himself out on the grass to dry, knew that Gallagher, like others whom he had saved from drowning in his time, was shocked and told him to call into their house on his way home: "Ask Sally, my sister, to wet you a bowl of tea. It will warm you up after the scare you have had today. See if she has a drop or two of brandy in the house, and drink some of it, too; it will help you to get over your fright and carry you safely home."

Gallagher's breathing returned to normal. He seemed angry that his theory about swimming was proved wrong, but most of all he was ashamed of not being able to swim and at having endangered Charley's life as well as his own. He may have been dreading the fact that news of his misadventure would travel all over the district before the same time on the following Sunday and that he would be jeered at by the young lads and by the old women.

When fully dressed Gallagher walked away without saying as much as a word of thanks to the brothers for having saved his life.

THE HAUNTED HOUSE

The MacWhirter family lived on a small hilly farm in Fanad. Their mother was dead. Peter, their father, was a stonemason by trade; and since the sites on which he worked, under contract, were many miles away, he was often absent from home for weeks at a time.

Most nights his children sat around the fire without any adult to keep them company. They often felt desolate and sorry for their lot in life.

"If only Mammy were alive," one of them would say on lonely nights, "we would be very happy!"

They missed their mother. But visits from friends and neighbours helped to pass the time, quickly and pleasantly, and, on such nights, when they did have visitors, they went to bed elated.

The MacWhirters hated the winter. For them it was the loneliest season of the year, because the mornings and nights were so unbearably long, cold, and dark. They dreaded the dark, but were unwilling to admit their dread to each other, their father, and their friends.

They were hard-working, tolerably brave, and trustworthy, and because of these excellent qualities their father was very proud of them. Like most children, they were proud of him; and of the tall and splendid buildings he built in North East Donegal.

The MacWhirter boys, with one exception, dreamed of being stonemasons and the girl talked to other girls about her determination to marry a builder when she came of age.

One evening the MacWhirters sat in front of the fire warming their hands. It was a particularly cold night in February: a gale was blowing from the south-west — making sinister, whistling sounds in the chimney; the rain fell torrentially and beat against the windows, making scratchy and other annoying and forlorn sounds.

The five youngsters were very weary of the night and were about to give up hope of having visitors, when, to their great joy and relief, the front door opened forcefully and Dan the Farmer pushed in from the dark and the storm.

His long, heavy overcoat in disarray, Dan stood motionlessly in the middle of the room looking directly at the fire and breathing loudly; water dripped intermittently from his coat and cap onto the flagged floor and a small pool of water marked where he stood.

Rising promptly and joyously Ellen MacWhirter addressed her visitor playfully:

"Goodnight Dan, you are welcome."

She went towards him.

"You are soaking wet!" she exclaimed. "Take your coat off before you catch cold; come up to the fire; Charles — get up and give your seat to Dan. Dan, put your cap on the crane — it will dry quickly over the fire, so it will."

Not until he was comfortably seated did Dan speak to them for the first time that night.

"Well, children, it is a rough and gusty night out there."

With a sigh and a melancholy shake of the head Dan continued speaking in his over-dramatic style.

"I would not take a pension for standing on top of the Rock of Cashel a night like this; it would be purgatory —

no mistake about it!"

"I agree. You would get the Limb-of-your-Death on any rock tonight, Dan," Johnny offered, knowingly.

Johnny MacWhirter was a puny child who liked to talk to adults; his mind was developed far beyond his chronological age. He had strange reading habits and read widely and used his increasing store of knowledge to show-off his learning before others, and because of this weakness, he was often taunted and ignored and his genius was not appreciated. His sister, in one of her fits of temper, told him frankly:

"Johnny, my darling brother, your tongue is the most prominent part of your anatomy; if it were just a wee bit longer, there is not a lawyer or politician in Ireland who could hold a candle to you for old chat and contention!"

Ellen MacWhirter was a good sister to her four brothers notwithstanding her conceit. She had a figure like a girl of nineteen but mentally she was still a child. She was a reasonably good housekeeper, an excellent cook, and her neighbours said that she took after her late mother for these gifts. She kept the house capitally, and knitted and sewed for her menfolk.

"Pull your chair closer to the fire," she told her visitor authoritatively. "You will catch a draught — you will catch pneumonia if you are not careful."

She remembered her mother's last illness and felt sorrowful. "That is what took Mammy's life, Dan!"

"It was, the poor woman," Dan said sadly.

"May God rest her soul," Ellen prayed, through tears.

"Amen," Dan added, reverently.

To hide her sorrow Ellen asked Dan to tell a ghost story.

Dan nodded. Even though he was a confirmed bachelor Dan was very fond of children, and treated them with great respect, affection, and understanding. He was fascinated by the earnestness and sweetness of this blue-eyed, dark-haired girl of fourteen, and could deny her nothing.

"Do surely Dan; tell us a couple of good ghost stories," little Micko shouted, gleefully, rubbing his tiny hands together and looking at his siblings for approval and support. "I love your stories and tales. Daddy says he never met a person who could beat you at that game. He says he does not know where you get them all. Where do you get them, Dan?"

"Ach! Can you not give the man time to draw his breath?" Johnny told Micko superciliously; "then he will tell yarns and fibs until we are blue in the face listening to them and be afraid to go to bed with fright! He should not tell such horrible stories at all, and we should not listen to his ghost stories; they are bad for the nerves and he only makes them up as he goes along!"

Johnny preferred histories, biographies, and science books to the frightening stories Dan, and other men, told around the fireside concerning the occult; he considered himself too wise, and his time too precious, to be wasting, listening to such utter nonsense; he read, leisurely and with careful attention, every book he could find, particularly if it dealt with the life of Bonny Prince Charley, the Battle of Culloden, and the plight and adventures of the Jacobite Clansmen following the defeat of the Stuart cause in 1745 and '46.

Because of his rudeness to Dan, Ellen scolded him:

"None of your old impudence in front of visitors. Too bad your precious books do not make a gentleman out of you as well as a scholar!"

She punished him by giving him a lively thump on the shoulder, which he endured without comment or action.

Meanwhile Dan was filling his pipe without the slightest show of haste. He lit it thoughtfully, and blew clouds of smoke across the room and up the chimney. Then he looked the living-room over, and said:

"I will tell you heaps of stories if you can put my mind at ease on a few points: is the house work, and the homework, done? And are the cows and horses and pigs fed? I trust you remembered to bring in sufficient turf and drinking water to last till morning!"

With much enthusiasm they submitted their reports to him, and, when they had satisfied him on these points, he began thus:

"Once upon a time there lived in Innisowen a family by the name of O'Codendiff. For many, many years these children were as good as gold: doing their homework, helping in and about the house and on the farm, running messages for their parents and elderly neighbours, saying their prayers, and doing all other sorts of good deeds.

"However, for no apparent reason they changed: refusing to run errands for others, they quarrelled frequently, stopped praying, and got into the bad habit of cursing, swearing, and sitting up late at night; and in no time at all their reputation for being unruly and cantankerous spread all over the peninsula.

"I often heard it said in my young days: evil is rewarded by evil! And so it was with the O'Codendiffs: a terrible curse and reprobation fell upon their heads and their home.

"One night, when Father and Mother O'Codendiff were out visiting sick relatives, their children were left to fend for themselves, for a couple of hours. No sooner had their parents gone out than these unruly children quarrelled, swearing like troopers, cursing like dragoons and creating such a hell of a racket, that its equal did not occur since the Siege of Derry.

"During the lull in the battle a loud band was heard in one of the upstairs rooms right above their heads; it was followed by an equally loud and odd rumpus. A rumpus I must hasten to say that frightened the daylights out of them, despite their toughness. They were cute enough to know that this noise was unearthly — so they downed tools and ran from the house as fast as their legs could carry them; they stopped running when they thought they were a safe distance away and stood looking back at the house, to see what would happen next —"

"What happened next?" Ellen said.

Dan spat into the fire, and replied:

"What do you think? Nothing much for a while; well, to continue:

"The O'Codendiffs were still gaping at the house when their parents returned. Of course Mr. & Mrs. O'Codendiff wondered what was the matter and asked their frightened children what was wrong at all; these children were too stunned to lie, so they told their parents all there was to be known. Together the ten O'Codendiffs approached their home, cautiously, and, while still a long way off, they could hear the rumpus. It continued unabated that night, and the next night, and the night after; so that, no one could get a wink of sleep.

"They quickly realised, of course, that their house was haunted; and some weeks later, finding no alternative, they sold their farm and went to live in London."

"What happened next?" Ellen said again.

Dan did not reply directly, but shook his head, spat again into the fire, and continued:

"Now, the man who bought the O'Codendiff farm was from Buncrana originally but for years he had been working and living in Clydebank, in Scotland. The O'Codendiffs were smart enough to tell nobody of their house being haunted, and it was not until the Buncrana man and his wife arrived with a view to occupying their new domain, that they learned the house was haunted; it was too late for going back on the deal. So, to make a long story short, they sent word to the local curate, telling him of their predicament and imploring him to come at once to bless the house and exorcise the evil spirit, who had it haunted."

"Did the priest banish the ghost," Tam asked, impatient to know the result. Tam was generally the silent type.

"Man dear, Tam, can you not wait till I tell the rear of it?" Dan said sternly.

"The priest came to visit them right away. He was a young, active sort of man. He was regarded, locally, as a bit of a football-fanatic. With a stole about his neck, a prayer book in one hand, a container of holy water in the other, he went about the ground floor, blessing the rooms, kitchen and bathroom. Next he went up stairs. The people of the house held their breaths and were wild with fright for his safety. Sure there was not a bother on the priest, no more than if he were going out on the field to play soccer for Carn. Rangers.

"Finally, he entered the ghost's room. He was there a short space of time only when he started prancing and frolicking like a two-year old calf.

"The man of the house thought the priest was kicking a football against the wall, while his wife thought the priest had suddenly gone mad or was defending himself against the ghost. Both of them ran to the bottom of the stairs, to see what the priest was doing on the landing. And what do you think they saw?"

Dan looked at each of the MacWhirters in turn with an inquisitive expression on his unshaven, weather-beaten, face.

The MacWhirters replied in unison: "Do not know; tell us, Dan."

"The priest was kicking a strange animal. This animal was larger and more ugly than a turkey-cock! The priest kicked this strange looking animal down the stairs and across the hall and outside, while, at the same time, shouting in an authoritative and pious manner:

" 'In the name of God, Satan, depart from this house, for ever and ever'!

"This animal, clothed in what looked like a mixture of hair and feathers, was no other ghost than the Devil himself, in disguise.

"It was a frightful spectacle to behold: the priest kicking the Devil across the yard. The priest took a long, strong chain from a cart in the shed and kicked the Devil down the garden towards a high circular rock, which stood in the midst of a clump of bushes — and tied the fiend to it, securely."

The MacWhirters did not speak while Dan filled his pipe again, and lit it slowly. They watched while he blew clouds of smoke about the room and up the chimney. Then, in a confidential manner, he ended the tale with the following epilogue:

"Thirty years have passed since the day the priest tied the Devil to the rock, in Innisowen. During all this time the Devil kept jumping against the chain trying to free himself, the chain cut into the rock, and all that is left of the ten-foot thick rock is a piece no thicker than your wrist. Some children on the peninsula cannot imagine what will happen on the day the chain cuts the whole way through the rock and the Devil is freed?

"Their parents kept telling them (and continue to tell them!) not to worry because God, who is good, will not let them come to any harm; rather, He will let the rock fall on the Devil as the fiend pulls free. Most likely the rock will hit the Devil on the head and cause a blister, the size of a chamber-pot, to rise on the side of his head; no doubt he will lose his memory; indeed, they hope so.

"The children of Innisowen are praying earnestly that the

whole unpleasant affair will end satisfactorily from their point of view; they are hoping that the rock will stun Satan — so that, not remembering who he is, or what he is, or where he is, but suffering from a splitting headache, the devil will wander aimlessly through Ireland until the consummation of the world!"

"I must admit," Johnny said, "that if you had a university education, and could write stories and have them published, you would become mighty rich and famous, Dan!"

"Thank you," Dan replied, pleased. "That is a compliment coming from you, Johnny MacWhirter. Since I am good at telling tales, and you are a good scribe, why don't we team up and publish our work; we could form a partnership and embark on a joint literary venture. 'Mac & Mac', how about that title for a tag, children?"

Before Johnny or any of her other brothers could reply, Ellen asked Dan to tell another story while his mouth was warm.

Dan told them the story of the drunken match-maker.

Ellen, busy preparing supper, listened intently; Tam shook his head and kept silent; Johnny read a comic-book entitled 'Red Rory of the Eagles'; little Micko went to sleep in the corner; and Charles went upstairs to bed and dreamt about priests, devils and haunted houses!

A HIGH TIDE

Some distance from the town of Moville lived a small farmer and part-time fisherman by the name of William MacDove. Locally he was known as Billy Bugle because his father, Andrew MacDove, played the bugle in an Orange Band. Billy himself learned to play the flute. When he developed blood-pressure the doctors advised him to change to some other instrument, preferably one which did not require so much wind, Billy opted to beat the drum in the Orange Band. He loved music, and, when the gramophone came out, Billy was the first person in his townland to acquire the machine together with fifty records of the finest music and song then on sale in Derry City.

Billy, who was born and reared a Presbyterian, did not attend Church for many years because he had ceased to believe many of its tenets, saying; "I do not believe God damned anyone from all eternity. He is a God of love. Judas damned himself through his greed of filty lucre. John Calvin may have been right about somethings in his day, but he was far off the mark in many things . . ." Strangely enough, Billy held the Catholic Church in high esteem; but, since Calvanism is begottedly anti-Catholic, Billy could neither bring himself to join a Church whose doctrines he was taught to hate when a youngster nor bring himself to abandon the Orange Order in which he had been steeped by tradition. Therefore he remained with a foot in both camps. In many respects he had the best of two worlds: courted by his Protestant neighbours, who wanted to keep him within the fold, and honoured by his Catholic neighbours because he did not scruple to attend funerals and retreats in the Catholic chapel.

Billy belonged to one of Derry's many Orange Lodges. From the beginning of June until the end of August, he attended training sessions and functions. The Lodge could boast of one of the best Flute Bands in Ulster. The fact that, through illness, Billy had been relegated from fluter to drummer did not in the least diminish his enthusiasm. He bought his own instrument and paid his occasional bus-fare and other incidental expenses out of his own pocket. It was an expensive hobby for a poor man, but it was as much as he could enjoy in life. Billy, who lived in a low thatched cottage on the Banks of the Foyle on the St. Johnstown side of Moville, got an occasional lift in Dicky Hutton's car. Dicky was a fluter in Billy's Bank and was a member of the Church of Ireland.

Billy never married. Although it was said that he courted girls before going off to the First World War, where he was slightly wounded in the leg from which he walked with a bit of a limp, he never read the newspapers or books. He always spoke highly of the genius and inventiveness of the Germans, against whom he had fought in France; and, when the local Presbyterian Minister, Rev. Mr Weathercock, asked him what he thought of Vatican II, Billy exclaimed:

"Holy smoke, Reverend Weathercock, have the Germans invented yet another machine-gun!"

About his war experience Billy seldom spoke. He loved to talk of three subjects: Farming, fishing and music. His little cottage was a rambling centre of the townland from the beginning of October until the end of April, when the sons and daughters of his Catholic neighbours gathered around his big fire of turf for a bit of crack. They loved Billy. To these youngsters he was dearer than many an uncle. Still, like all other youngsters of Donegal, they could be rather cruel towards him in certain respects. For instance, when another Twelfth of July drew near, they resolved to play a prank on Billy. They waited until the eve of the Twelfth before climbing onto the roof of his little cottage and placing a bucket of water on the kitchen chimney. From the handle of the bucket they let down a grass rope. The rope reached a little bit short of the brace. Billy, they knew, was sound asleep in the far end of the cottage. He always went to bed early in order to be well rested for walking and drumming in the Orange Parade the next day in Derry City.

The Twelfth dawned with a rather gusty breeze. Billy built a blaze in the fire-place and set a pandy of water on the turf. While he awaited the boiling of the water for his tea he sat before the fire and lit his pipe. It was after he had blown a few columns of smoke up the chimney that he saw the rope. Thinking that it had been blown off the roof by the wind during the night, Billy pulled the rope in order to get it away from the fire, and, as he pulled, the bucket — as it was supposed to do — spilled its contents down the chimney, put out the fire, and spilled the pandy of water.

"Holy smoke!" Billy exclaimed, shocked. Before he could get the fire re-kindled and have more water brought to the boil for his breakfast, a colleague in the Orange Band, Dicky Hutton, blew the horn. Together they drove to the Parade's assembly point in Derry City. Soon the sun was high in the sky and the breeze disappeared. Billy beat the drum, Dicky blew the flute. In every respect it was a grand day. Their fellow Orangemen looked smart and fit with their stylish suits, bowler hats, and their colourful sashs, which had come down to them from generation to generation; there was little or no stone-throwing by the young Papists of Derry, and, all in all, it was the kind of day which made a Presbyterian feel glad that he was still a Protestant and a loyal brother of the Order in yet another celebration of William III's victory over the bigotted Catholic king, James II, at the Battle of the Boyne in 1690, when Britain was saved from Popish slavery.

Following several hectic hours of marching and playing Billy, Dicky, and the other bandsmen retired to a public house for a beer, a smoke, and a chat. When drinks were served and Billy and Dicky had seated themselves into a quiet corner, Dicky took a large slug of beer and Billy lit his pipe. Says Dicky:

"Fine day, Billy; it's about the best Twelfth we've had in years." He licked his lips with satisfaction. "A bit hot though, too hot in fact; there's not an air; what a pity the sharp morning breeze fizzled out; still in all, it was a bit too breezy when we were coming up the road this morning."

Billy nodded as he blew smoke across the room. "Aye, he

said contentedly, "it was windy all right." Then, remembering the prank the sons of his Papist neighbours had played on him, he added with a smile:

"There was a high tide this morning!"

Dicky, who had no knowledge of the prank, did not know why Billy was talking about a high tide, but then Billy often said strange things. They began discussing music and now and then members of the Band would approach for a chat and to offer to buy them a drink. Dicky would politely refuse, saying:

"I'm driving, lads; you may stand Billy another beer if you like. Thanks all the same."

Since Billy refused nothing, by the time Dicky pulled into Billy's farm-yard Billy was senseless with drink. "Poor fellow," said Dicky as he carried him inside and laid him full stretch on the bed," you'd be sober if you had a wife and eight children and drove a car all the way from Derry City." Then he went home and told his wife about Billy being a drunken disgrace to the Protestant community on yet another marvellous Twelfth of July.

The next morning Billy awoke early with a splitting headache and longed for a high tide to carry him out to sea and put him out of his misery on yet another Thirteenth of July.

THE THREE GRAVES

Not far from the White Strand there were three graves. The fishermen of long ago knew exactly where they were located and whose corpses lay resting in them.

It was the custom until recent times for farmers to gather seaweed for fertiliser on moonlit nights. For some reason, none of the farmers living adjacent to the White Strand would risk gathering the seaweed on his own. It was said by the local fishermen that every farmer who ever tried to gather seaweed on this strand at night was compelled to abandon the enterprise speedily.

It was not until the MacCallan brothers went there to gather seaweed for their turnips that people gained some idea what had made loners abandon the gathering of seaweed on what was a relatively safe beach. If the loners had been mute regarding their experience, one of the MacCallan brothers was not silent about his own experience: Here is James MacCallan's account of what transpired:

"It was the night following St Patrick's Day. The moon was high, the sky clear, and there was not a breath of wind. John and I left home at eleven o'clock and reached the White Strand a little after twelve.

Since the storm had washed heaps of wreck ashore, we worked like madmen for two hours carrying the seaweed out of reach of the tide and stacking it conveniently, for the horse and cart. Then we ate a sandwich and smoked the pipe.

Soon after going back to work, I saw a light out in the Lough. John did not see it. It came towards us, and, although I could not see any boat, the light went in at the far end of the strand, and continued up the sand dunes.

As soon as the light disappeared, the air became bitterly cold; we were forced to jump about and clap our hands together in order to keep warm; this cold lasted for a quarter of an hour. When the cold went away the air became unbearably hot. The cold air did not surprise us, but the heat was abnormal for that time of night or year. We felt weak from the heat and could not work except wipe the perspiration off our brows.

Says I to John: 'It's very hot.'

John replied: 'I don't like it; I feel like going in for a dip to cool myself.'

The night returned to normal and we went to our work for a while before I began to notice an aery feeling. John noticed it too. Says he to me:

'James, I'm afraid. There's a ghostly presence, I feel it.'

We grew so terrified that we could not move a muscle. 'Look, look, James,' John whispered, 'do you see the three men coming down the grazing?'

I looked at the sand dunes, and sure enough three sailors were marching, one after the other, down towards the water less than twenty yards from where we stood.

'I see them,' I told John; 'they must have come in with the light.'

'See what they're doing,' John said surprised, 'they are walking into the water!'

The three sailors walked until the water was up to their waists. Says I to John: 'Do they want to drown themselves?'

John did not speak. He was watching them intently with a frightened expression on his face. I looked back at the sailors, who were now up to their shoulders in the water.

'Come back, men, or you'll drown?' John shouted a warning.

Ignoring him, they continued until the water covered them all over.

'God Almighty!' John exclaimed, 'what will we do, James? We can't let them drown themselves?'

At this point I remembered the three graves. I pulled John by the arm: 'Come on,' I said, 'those sailors drowned when the Saldahna sank in 1811. They're ghosts!'

John and I dropped our tools, reached for our coats, and

ran like hares up the sand dunes; we did not stop running until we were half a mile away from the White Strand. Our shirts were sticking to our backs with perspiration, and it also ran down our faces like rain.

Having reached home in record time, we lit the fire, boiled the kettle, and made ourselves some punch to drive the weariness out of our bones and to steady our nerves. Then we went to bed, out of which John never stirred, for he died a week later.

The doctor said John died from pneumonia, but I say he died of fright!"

THE DROWNING

Tam got off his bicycle at the stone bridge. The bridge was crowded with people of all ages. They were very excited and milling about, and shouting: asking questions and making conjectures; boys and girls stood on the bridge's broad parapet looking into the river.

Tam could not see what was attracting their attention so intently. At first, he thought, quite naturally, that some men, members of some local club, perhaps, were giving a swimming and diving exhibition; what else could be engaging the attention of such a large crowd?

Tam was an easy-going sort of fellow. He leaned against the bar of his bicycle, which was a Raleigh model, in a resting position; he was in no particular hurry and he felt like having a bit of a rest after pushing his bicycle up steep hilly roads; and, in any event, he liked watching diving and swimming exhibitions and sports of all kinds.

An old man was standing closeby smoking a big, crooked-headed Peterson pipe; he was trying, with some difficulty and exertion, to avoid the surge of the crowd. Once or twice,

Tam noticed, the old man was pushed, and almost losing his balance, staggered, and gained balance clumsily.

"This is a terrible spot to be in!" the old man told Tam in a friendly, familiar manner.

Tam had never seen the old man before in his life and felt sure the old man was seeing Tam for the first time, also; he was just being neighbourly.

"They are dragging the river, now, for Podge O'Rourke; they say he is drowned —"

"What happened?" Tam ventured to ask.

The old man took a long and significant pull at his pipe, blew smoke out of one side of his toothless mouth, and spoke, solemnly:

"Podge O'Rourke, I am told, was passing over the bridge, here, on his way to Mass, when he heard a splash in the river, it was followed by a child's cry for help. Johnny MacCrawford was with him, at the time."

The old man stopped, took another great pull at his pipe, puffed the smoke out his broad nostrils, and continued:

"They went over to the parapet, looked into the river, to see what was happening there, blimmy, there were two children, belonging to Rump O'Hanlon, struggling in the water. The children are aged from four to six years of age; they could not swim.

"Podge pulled off his shoes and jacket and hopped into the river. A good swimmer was Podge — a strong swimmer. He managed, with the help of Johnny, operating from the bank, to get the two O'Hanlon lads out alive, but, a cramp or something like a cramp must have hit him, because, according to Johnny's version of the story, Podge fell back into the river when he tried to climb onto the bank; he sank, of course, and, before you could say 'do not get wet', he was a gonner! He —"

"Poor fellow!" Tam exclaimed with regret. "He will be sure to get into Heaven for saving the children. Dammit it all, it was too bad, too bad, entirely!"

Tam was religious, and many of his friends regarded him as quite a sentimentalist.

"Too bad! God rest his soul!" Tam muttered. "Too bad, what a pity."

" 'Tis mind you," the old man agreed. "But the getting into Heaven part of it . . . well, I do not know about that: Podge was into every kind of mischief — he was; do you understand me now?" the old man confided. "He kept his poor mother fretting and worrying, by his outrageous activities. The Guards were always after him; if not for one offence, then for another. Sure they were! I remember the time — only a few years back, when Podge and a handful of mates — every man-jackass of them fit for anything middling! — killed a tinker's pony . . ."

The old man searched his pockets and brought out a delapidated match box, opened it, and exclaimed:

"Damn it all! — not a match left." He threw the box away with a swift flick of his burly, dirty hand, and, turning to Tam, asked pleasantly: "Would you have a match to spare, like a good man?"

Tam produced a new box of safety matches. The old man took them greedily.

"Good man, good man," he said sharply and turned his back to the wind and cracked a match and began lighting his pipe with gusto. He was pushed a little by the crowd but managed admirably to set up a splendid chain of smoke clouds.

"I am always short of matches these days; the tobacco nowadays is not worth a shit," he told Tam between puffs.

Tam laughed.

"I will tell you now, Podge O'Rourke, and his pals — the MacBartons, O'Pillons and MacSharkeys and them lads: they could not keep their hands to themselves, they would have to be doing depredation of one kind or another; they would surely, villains," the old man said and made an obscene gesture with his fingers. "Now, take the killing of the pony for instance —"

Some one pushed against Tam and he almost fell with his bicycle. The old man said:

"Get back, lads, do not tumble a stranger. Get back or that!" He pushed some lads back and helped Tam resume equilibrium.

". . . Podge and his cohorts gave this district a bad name, with their throwing stones at passing cars, at telegraph poles

and street lights; shouting filthy slogans and other innuen-
does at visitors, women, and harmless old people."

The old man shook his head sadly.

"They seem to be a tough bunch?" Tam commented.

"Blimmy so they are; but, behind it all, they are bloody
cowards. You often heard it said, and it is true, 'the greater
the criminal the greater the coward'. Podge's drowning will
have a sobering effect upon them, I am thinking, because he
was a ring-leader."

The old man broke off his monologue and exclaimed: "Ah!
Blimmy . . . they have him up at last!"

There was a rush from one end of the bridge to the other,
and a certain stillness came over the crowd. The old man
pushed his way through the crowd to the parapet and put his
head between two small boys. In his haste he almost caused
them to lose their balance and fall into the river. He leaned
over the parapet and shouted various comments, for Tam's
benefit.

"Come here young fellow," he beseeched Tam.

Tam was a reserved sort of fellow — not at all pushy; he
stayed where he was, because it would have meant pushing
his way forward; with the bicycle such an action would be
awkward and create ill-feeling among the spectators on the
parapet; and, besides, he had no real wish to look at the body
of someone who had died from drowning — he knew he had
no stomach for such a gruesome sight. He thought Podge's
corpse would be distorted. He had heard it said, that, 'when a
person dies by drowning, the body becomes swollen with
water'. He did not care to see any such sight.

Meanwhile the old man came over to Tam and motioned
with his hands.

"Come right over to the parapet and see the affair," he
ordered. "It is perhaps your first time to witness such an
accident, you might never see another drowning tragedy.
Come right over here."

Tam hesitated. The old man was back at the parapet,
where boys and girls were now quarrelling — each one trying
to obtain an advantageous position, from which to watch the
activities below in the river and on the bank of the river. The
old man took his cap off, and, using it as a weapon, beat

wildly, hitting boys and girls on the neck and shoulders and head. They reluctantly retreated under his attack shouting protests and obscene words.

"Now young fellow! Here is enough space for your bicycle and yourself."

Under normal conditions, Tam would have laughed at the old man's antics; instead, he was slightly embarrassed by the old man's behaviour; however he moved over the parapet with a certain amount of reluctance.

Down below, on the far bank, a group of sturdy men were gathered. Two men, dressed in swim-suits, were in the water, and two others were lying flat on their bellies, pulling the body up from the river. As they dragged it up onto the river bank, a mighty sigh went up from the crowd; and some women sobbed and uttered laments.

Tam withdrew from the parapet. For a while he felt physically sick; cold beads of perspiration rolled down his face, and he wanted to get away from the scene as quickly as possible.

The crowd began to melt away.

Tam and the old man moved slowly down the road and after a lengthy silence, the old man said:

"Blimmy that is the way: here yesterday, gone today!"

"Dammit, it is tough on the O'Rourkes," Tam said, compassionately.

The old man nodded and was silent. After a while, he asked Tam would he care for a drink. This took Tam completely by surprise.

"Is there a pub in the village?" Tam asked automatically; he liked drink once in a while and thought he needed a whisky to steady his nerves.

"Blimmy, Ireland is adequately supplied with public-houses and churches," the old man asserted.

Again they were silent. They walked along, each man thinking his own brand of thoughts.

"Poor Podge! Blimmy he will not be playing football, or swimming, or acting the micky, from now on — not here anyway; it will be a great shock to Cormac, in England. Cormac is a brother of the deceased," the old man explained.

"Aye, it will be a shock, all right," Tam understood such

things.

"Cormac is a Holy Father, a Carmelite — I think You know the lads who grow beards and wear brown habits?"

"They are Capuchins," Tam surmised.

"You are probably right on the nail. Well blimmy Cormac will be coming home for the funeral. He will be a comfort to his widowed mother; he will, blimmy. Terrible news for a young man to be getting. I knew Cormac since he was a blighter going to school, always obliging — more than I can say for the deceased. Ah, I should not be saying uncharitable things about the dead?"

The old man was repentant.

They were at the nearest public house. It was a detached house, and Tam got the impression that the public-house was once a busy hotel. The old man went first and opened the door and led the way to the counter. Tam shut the door.

The bar was literally crowded. A cloud of thick tobacco smoke floated about their heads, as if it were searching for an exit.

Tam walked up and stood beside the old man and was conscious of the silence which came over the room on their entry.

"What are you having?" the old man asked Tam when the barman came to take their orders.

"A glass of Powers," Tam told the old man. The latter asked for a bottle of beer for himself and whisky for Tam.

"Righto, Mr MacClogher," the barman said casually and fixed their drinks. "That was an unfortunate accident up there at the river this morning!" The barman spoke over his shoulder, and added: "Were you up on the bridge when they recovered the body?"

"We were, blimmy," the old man said gloomily.

"For a strong swimmer like Podge O'Rourke, I cannot understand what went wrong. After all is said and done, the water could not have been that cold for the month of October? Some say he had a weak heart; the same complaint that killed old man O'Rourke."

"I suppose he had a big breakfast and was walking fast and sweating. It is easy, they say, to get cramp in the water if you are hot going in, or have a full stomach!" Tam said authoritatively. Tam learning to swim, was a diver of some merit.

The barman looked sharply at Tam, and said.

"I do not think we have been introduced?"

"My name is Tam O'Shanahan. I am a first cousin to Tom MacSweeney, of Shadenstown, two miles from here. I suppose you know Tom and his brother, Jack?"

"I do not know Tom hardly at all because he does not drink, I believe; but I certainly know Jack very well. He is one of my regulars . . . comes in here at weekends but he has not been in here this month — he has a blood-poisoned hand, I believe? Well, I am glad to meet a cousin of Jack's," the barman said and reached his hand across the counter, and added: "The name is MacFeigh."

"Dammit I am glad to meet you, MacFeigh," Tam said and shook the barman's bony hand.

The old man also shook Tam's hand. "You know my name? — It is MacClogher; I used to be a black Protestant before I turned with the Mrs. Now I am nothing much — neither Prod nor Pap!"

Tam did not know what to say to that, and decided to let the remark pass without commenting. The barman went to serve other customers; the old man was thoughtful, again. He took a sip of beer and licked his thin lips but failed, Tam noticed, to collect the drops which hung from the ends of his grey moustache; eventually he said:

"That the first drowning tragedy you have had the misfortune to witness? What age are you? — if that is not a vulgar question? I would say you are over thirty . . ."

Tam took a mouthful of whisky, swallowed hastily and replied:

"I will be thirty-six come February next."

"Blimmy, sure you are the very age I was when I went off to the war! I was in France and Belgium fighting the Hun. A tough fighter is the Hun; but in the end we were beating him good and proper. The old Kaiser was not a bad blighter, just a bit of a nut-case! He had the best army in the world; left to himself he would have beaten either the British Army, or the French Army, or the Russian Army, or —"

The old man took another sip of beer.

". . . He was a bit of a blighter — the Kaiser was — and, a bit of a braggart! He said his soldiers were the salt of the earth; they were that indeed —"

"Is that so?" Tam asked with interest.

"Blimmy yes; that was well known. The Kaiser was a sound man in many ways. Hitler is a Charley Chaplin in comparison with the old Kaiser. He was fighting on half a dozen fronts: Russia, France, Belgium, Italy, Rumania, and . . let me see now? . . . where else? . . . yes, Poland, aye and Serbia, and —"

"I have often heard them talking about the Kaiser, Paddy MacJohnson had a horse he called the Kaiser," Tam said with swagger; he ordered another round for both of them.

The old man talked eloquently of his war days. Tam was interested in history and listened with steadfast attention. They drank several rounds. The old man grew silent and Tam began to talk; loudly at first but hesitantly, then freely and entirely unrestrained when the drink began to go to his head. Drink always had had this effect on him. He lost his inhibitions and talked so loudly and interestingly, that the other customers in the public-house stopped all conversation and began to give him their ears . . .

The old man looked at the clock on the wall, excused himself and went out to the toilet. Returning to the room, he shook Tam's hand and went home.

Tam was merry.

When the old man was gone, Tam inquired about his family.

"The old man is Podge O'Rourke's uncle on the mother's side of the house," the barman said.

Tam was sober enough to be surprised. "Why did he not mention that fact to me?"

"Well, it is a long story," the barman began; "you see, old man O'Rourke was Captain of the local I.R.A. during the Troubles and married MacClougher's sister, Lizzy. She changed her religion with O'Rourke. She has remained a practising Catholic to this day. MacClogher never turned with his wife — he just lets on he did; do you twig me now?"

"I do," Tam acknowledged with a blurred voice.

"MacClogher was in the Royal Navy and was thrown out of it because he was accused of killing another sailor. A fight over a woman. When he left the navy, he joined the Black-

and-Tans. He was as pro-British as they come, and so was his father before him. In the Tans he was a hard man, I am told. Young Podge, brought up a staunch Republican by his father, disliked his uncle because of the anti-Irish part he played during the Troubles; and there was always bad blood between the two; do you twig me now?"

"I do indeed, MacFeigh," Tam said; but in truth he was quite confused, and, leaving immediately, he mounted his bicycle and peddled unsteadily down the road.

HOLY AMBITION

". . . Please go to sleep, son," Mrs O'Sheridan told her eight year old grandson compassionately.

"No, granny, I cannot," little Colum replied. "I am fretting about mammy. Is she . . . is she going to get well?" He held her cold hand for comfort.

Mrs O'Sheridan could barely contain her tears because her daughter, Catherine, the little Column's mother, who lay unconscious in the next room — surrounded by relatives and attended by Dr O'Harkin — had, a few days before, been delivered of another still-born baby, and her life now hung in this world as delicately as a thin woollen thread.

Mrs O'Sheridan looked at her favourite grandson and decided to be frank because it seemed to her the sensible thing to do in the circumstances.

"Your mammy is very ill, Colum! She has given birth to a still-born baby — a little girl, your sister. Although you are still a child, you can imagine how sad she was about losing her baby . . ."

At last, tears ran down the old woman's wrinkled, reddish face: she remembered the look of despair which appeared on Catherine's ashen face when the mid-wife, Nurse MacHagan, told her that her fifth child had been still-born and to add to the sadness of the occasion Freddy, Catherine's sailor-husband, was at sea somewhere in the region of the Mediter-

ranean. If he were at home on leave, Mrs O'Sheridan thought,
Catherine would not be taking the matter so much to heart . .

"What did they call my sister?" little Colum wanted to
know.

Mrs O'Sheridan drew a flabby hand across her face and
suppressed a sob with difficulty. Her grandson's question had
pulled at the cords of her heart. She was a sentimental person.

"Your sister was not christened," Mrs O'Sheridan said
with some hesitation. "But we shall always refer to her as
"Heather" because she was born in June — the month when
the heather blossoms. We could not give her a saint's name
because she died without Baptism; she will never get into
Heaven, like your sister, Joan, but will remain in Limbo for
ever and ever, where your brothers are, son." Mrs O'Sheridan
reflected.

"Do I have brothers in Limbo?" Little Colum asked with
much seriousness and amazement. "What were my brothers'
names?"

Mrs O'Sheridan realised with regret that she had just told
him a secret: it had slipped out before she was aware of what
she was saying. "It does not really matter," she thought, "because he is inquisitive and intelligent and would have found
out, sooner or later, about his mother's other miscarriages."

"I suppose we called them something or other; I do not
remember and it really does not matter; they are —"

Little Colum looked thoughtful, and interjected with:
"Then I have a sister in Heaven, two brothers and one sister
in Limbo? — will I meet them in the next life? — will I see
them on the Day of Judgement, Granny?" His questions were
pathetic and yet, Mrs O'Sheridan knew, he must be answered
truthfully.

Overcoming her emotion Mrs O'Sheridan said matter-of-
factly: "Some day, when you are a priest, you will understand these mysteries; but, until then, Colum, a Stor, be a
good boy and go to sleep, for your poor old Granny is very
tired and very sad. You do not understand how sorrowful it
is for a mother to bring still-born children into the world.
Your mother is very depressed. When you are a priest you
will understand all of these things, dear child."

Since Colum was serving Mass on Sundays and Holidays,

and was a great one for books and prayers, his family and friends took it for granted he would take Holy Orders when he grew up.

"Granny, are the children in Limbo, happy? How do we know that there is such a place as Limbo? — where is it, then?" little Colum asked earnestly. Mrs O'Sheridan was surprised and shocked.

"Do not tell me, Colum MacShane, that you question the existence of Limbo, or ask where it is! The Church believes in Limbo, that is good enough for me and, sure our Holy Father says there is a place or state in the next life called Limbo, of course —"

"Did Pope Pius say there is a place or state in the next world, called Limbo? — what is it like, did he say, Granny? Are the children there, happy? — are they, Granny? Please say they are — are they?" He was pleading now, and looking full of foreboding.

"Has some one been telling you things, son, unpleasant things maybe? Have they, son? Ah, a Stor, I think I understand how you feel. You are kindness itself; you are merciful; you would not be wanting God to be punishing your brothers and sister for having died without Baptism, would you now? I know how you feel . . ." Tears built up in the kind old woman's amber-coloured eyes.

"I heard Fr MacCallain saying, that children in Limbo are much happier than we could be on earth, but their happiness is far from being as great and complete as that enjoyed by the Blessed in Heaven!" little Colum said with delight.

"So! — you are no heretic after all; you knew all along that Limbo existed for sure. You heard Fr MacCallain saying so, and you know he speaks truly. Well, are you not a wee rascal, to be worrying your old Granny —"

"Fr MacCallain said that Purgatory and Limbo are not mentioned specifically in the New Testament, but Jesus said: 'In my Father's Kingdom there are many mansions; if it were not so, I would have told you so'. Fr MacCallain said it is on this part of scripture the Catholic Church based her belief in Purgatory and Limbo."

"Well look at that, you are more than bright!"

Mrs O'Sheridan was naturally proud of her grandson's

learning and intelligence. She gave him a slight stroke of her hand on the cheek, and said:

"That is what the bishop will be doing with you when he gives you Confirmation next year." She tried to put merriment into her words but failed because she vividly remembered the agony her favourite daughter was going through in the next room — fighting for her life, fighting what seemed to be a losing battle. Dr O'Harkin had told Catherine after her first still-born baby arrived, that the risk of child-birth would be greater in future. Catherine and her young, irresponsible husband had taken chances time and time again, and now — now she was paying dearly for their cupidity — such, the old woman knew, was the power of love and the desire for conjugal union! Men — especially ignorant men — were selfish.

Mrs O'Sheridan disliked her son-in-law; from the moment she had met him she had done her utmost to have Catherine married off to the local doctor (Dr O'Harkin's predecessor), and, when this failed to materialise — because the doctor did not think Catherine good enough for him, she had looked around at the local schoolmaster, inviting him to the house and that sort of thing, all very discreetly arranged, but he, too, passed a good girl over and married Mrs MacSweeney's younger daughter, Linda, a flighty girl who was always leading the master around by the nose and making his life a misery; with Catherine he would have found an ideal wife, but Catherine never gave Master O'Calpin any encouragement and openly allowed herself to be wooed by an illiterate and uncouth sailor. "Only I loved her", Mrs O'Sheridan remembered, "I would have thrown her out of the house at the time, I felt so very bitter and disappointed . . ."

"I have prayed for Mammy," little Colum told Mrs O'Sheridan with confidence; "I have prayed for her recovery. God will cure her, sure he will, Granny?" He wanted to be reassured that God would hear and answer his prayers.

"Yes, I hope so; He will, Colum, if it is His Holy Will. Remember always, son, that God hears our prayers but he does not always answer them in the way we expect, because He alone knows what is best for us; He loves us more than any one else could ever love us, and for this reason He will grant our requests if He sees they are not going to interfere with our eternal happiness." She sighed, wishing her grandson would fall asleep and let her get to bed; there was much work to be done in cleaning and cooking and one ought to be fresh and rise early in the morning.

"Please tell me a story," little Colum demanded. "Then I will go to sleep, Granny!"

Mrs O'Sheridan sighed again. Little Column was so very earnest in his request, and was so eager to hear her tell a story, that she could not refuse. 'Poor child', she thought, 'with your father far away at sea, and your darling mother on the brink of death, you are to be pitied, my darling grandson . . .'

"Tell me a story about Jesus or the Saints. When I am a priest I would like to be able to tell people nice stories like the stories you read for me. Fr MacCallain tells nice stories, too, like you do, Granny; he tells them on the altar and to me afterwards in the sacristy."

Despite her tiredness Mrs O'Sheridan could not refuse; she thought how nice it would be for the family to have a priest, to pray for its members and, especially to pray for her own soul when she was dead and suffering for her sins in Purgatory. It is holy talk and holy stories, that inspires young boys to become priests, she believed, because she had heard it said by men who were in a position to know.

"Son, I will read you a beautiful story and when you are a priest, telling it to your parishioners, please remember the soul of your dear old Granny and ask them to pray with you for the repose of her soul —"

"I will surely, Granny! — I will never forget you," he said fervently. "I will never forget you or Heather, or my two brothers, or Joan, or mammy and daddy, or "

"Or your Gran-Daddy, Aunt Teresa and your other deceased relatives," Mrs O'Sheridan interjected with equal fervour She could see him in her mind's eye: see him sitting in the confessional listening to sinners confessing their sins to God; she could see him offering up the sacrifice of the Mass; she could see him baptising children — and he remembering, no doubt, two brothers and a sister who had not received the promise of life everlasting in the waters of Baptism; she could see him anointing the sick — like Fr MacCallain had anointed his mother yesterday; she could see him —"

"What story are you going to read, Granny?"

Mrs O'Sheridan took a book off the top of a wardrobe, fingered the pages and began reading the abridged edition of the biography of St Jean Vianney. When she had finished she closed the book, and said:

"Well, did you like St Jean . . .? There was no reply, for little Colum had fallen asleep. "God bless you, son?" she whispered lovingly and, bowing low over the child, kissed him fondly on the cheek. For a moment he reminded her of her own child, Frank, who had died on her knee at the age of three, many years before. She stood up and watched little Colum and wondered would he, too, be a priest like St Jean Vianney, or a seaman like his father?

"Perhaps," she said in a whisper, "you will be a priest with the help of God; but son, whatever calling you follow in life I trust you will remain faithful to God's Commandments, and that He will keep you from danger . . ."

Behind her pious intentions, Mrs O'Sheridan had an inflexible but holy ambition: she wanted to have it to say, that she had a grandson in the priesthood. Her cousin, Mrs O'Reilly, whom she disliked, had a son and a nephew in the Carmelites and Jesuits respectively, and was continuously bragging about their merits, their Orders, and so on. It would be nice having a photograph of Colum, dressed in his cassock, hanging over the mantle-piece in the living-room, and to be able to say, in answering questions put by neighbours.

"That priest there? Oh, that is my grandson, Colum; he is a Dominican Friar. The Dominicans were founded by St Dominic; he was a Spaniard, you know!"

Mrs O'Sheridan tip-toed out of her Grandson's room, went past his mother's room, into the kitchen and put the kettle on the fire. She poured a cup of tea and was sitting rather sleepily at the side table drinking tea when Dr O'Harkin knocked and entered.

"Mrs O'Sheridan," he said softly, he came forward and stood beside her, without speaking, as if he were going to communicate some remote or obscure medical phenomenon to a large audience.

"How is she, doctor?" Mrs O'Sheridan asked automatically.

"Is she improved? — anything . . . improved?"

Dr O'Harkin put his hand on her shoulder in a kindly manner. This was the disagreeable part of being a physician - one had to communicate unpleasant news. "Catherine has left us for a better world," he whispered. "My sympathy, Mrs O'Sheridan, is with you all. If there is anything I can do, please do not hesitate to let me know, Mrs O'Sheridan, anything —"

Mrs O'Sheridan crossed herself solemnly. "May God be good to her and rest her soul," she said reverently. "It is the will of God, Doctor, sure we did all we could for her. May she rest in peace and be with God in Heaven."

"Amen," the doctor replied. Then he went out quietly.

When he was gone, Mrs O'Sheridan, going over to the cupboard, took out a bottle of brandy and poured some of its contents into the tea-cup, and drank greedily. She felt for Freddy; for the first time in her life, she felt less antipathy towards him. It was strange — that feeling, but it was real.

"I must tell Colum; I must tell wee Colum and write a letter — no! — send a cablegram to Freddy. Dear Lord, I am mixed up . . . what will I do, how am I to reach Freddy . . .?"

She walked out off the kitchen and into Colum's room, where she stood looking at the sleeping figure for a considerable length of time.

"Colum," she said gently; but immediately she regretted what she was doing and retreated to the door of his room. "Colum, forgive me," she whispered. "Tomorrow will be soon enough to tell you . . . soon enough to tell you that you are an orphan."

Then she went out and quietly shut the door.

WHAT PAT SAW

It was my privilege as a stonemason to travel around County Donegal in the performance of my trade. I built dwelling-houses, barns, byres, stables, schools, chapels, garages, bridges, break-waters and sheds. I spent five years in the company of several masters before going out on my own account as a master mason, and for the next twenty years I met many other men of wide experience and versed in folklore, but not one person told me such an incredible tale as did Pat O'Friel. From personal experience Pat believed in the existence of faeries!

In my youth I was not interested in the other side of life because I thought I possessed too much good sense to know that faeries did not exist. I was a sceptic. I was sceptical because I read books on serious subjects, and from a deep study of the history of science, I had become convinced that talk about the occult was based on fiction.

I was a Christian; thus I believed in spirits as such, namely, devils of Hell, angels of Heaven and the souls of the dead generations of man; but I did not believe that the seeing of ghosts was a usual occurrence; certainly I did not believe in faeries. I was convinced that they were the invention of the novelist. I often listened patiently out of respect for the sensitive feelings of neighbours, friends, fellow workers while they told tales of ghosts and faeries.

These tales were told around the fireside on long, cold, windy winter nights and I was tolerant enough to consider such tale-telling a form of entertainment in much the same way as films about Cowboys and Indians I used to see, when

I was working in Drummullan, Letterglinchey and other large villages and towns, were entertaining.

"There is a simple scientific explanation for ghosts and faeries," I said when asked what I thought of such and such a story. When people pressed me for a further comment I would say: "Anyone who sees a ghost, or faery, cannot be in a sane state of mind; he must be drunk, or dreaming, or hallucinating, or suffering from a dangerous mental derangement, or is a saint . . ."

"Then, Dano, you do not believe in the Banshee so?"

People used to say I was not serious; they thought I was joking or trying their tempers. I was often told off — aye, and called a thick, and a pagan who believed in nothing — that I was inviting trouble from ghosts and faeries by mocking people who did believe. And, when I would get up from the fireside they would tell me I should be careful of the old Nick on my way home; they would say:

"Dano, keep a close look out for the Banshee and faeries . . . ."

I laughed and went about my business unconcernedly. I suppose some of those good but simple people wished that a ghost or faery would appear to me, letting off loud, terrifying cries, so that I would be frightened and taught a lesson not to be incredulous. Sometimes they went to great pains to rid me of my scepticism and to convince me of the existence of ghosts and faeries and to vindicate their own strongly-held beliefs . . .

"The faeries were the 'fallen angels'," an educated relative once explained. "When the war was raging in Heaven between God and Lucifer the majority of angels took sides but there was a minority which stood aside taking no act or part in the fight. And so when the war was over, and God and the good angels having won, and had expelled Lucifer and the bad angels, God punished the angels who had remained uncommitted; He cast them out of Heaven; they fell upon the earth where they must remain until the Day of Judgement, when they will be readmitted . . ."

I did not quite understand this theological assertion. I read books on the fall of Lucifer and the fall of Man to see if there was any truth in this man's assertion; but in most books the

term 'fallen angel' meant the Devil and his angels who are in
Hell for all eternity. I deduced therefore that there was no
such creatures as faeries — not, of course, in the form
mentioned by my learned relative. If some creatures did exist
— generally referred to in Ireland as 'Faery' or 'Shee', they
were, perhaps, the souls of unbaptised children, the souls of
the ancient pagans and their druids, the Tuatha De Dannan
and their descendants. In fact, I tried to reason the existence
of faeries; if they did exist, were they the De Dannan? I
remembered the flight of the defeated De Dannan to the
woods upon their defeat by an invader, where they lived in
caves and little wooden huts.

You see, the Tuatha De Dannan were small of stature,
were pagan, and were supposed to be familiar with the art of
witchcraft. It has been said of the Tuatha De Dannan that
they were pagans who were able to cast spells on enemies and
create mirages and storms; that, when they sighted the Celts
approaching the Shores of Erin they caused a dense fog to
fall over the sea, then they caused a storm to blow up, and,
when the Celts succeeded in landing, they created mirages
which confused the invader for a time. But, unfortunately for
the De Dannan, the Celts, seeing through the tactics of the
De Dannan, got their own druids and magicians to use
magical powers against the Natives — thus rendering the
magical powers of the De Dannan negative in effect, and,
when this battle of magic was over the two tribes met in
bloody confrontation and the De Dannan were routed. They
lived in the caves and woods of Ulster, married, begot children to whom they passed on their arts. They could make
themselves invisible, turn rocks into castles, trees into cabins,
benweeds into horses, and so on.

Yet, on religious grounds I could not subscribe whole-
heartedly to any such rationale. I was still sceptical. But I
kept searching for a more acceptable answer and at last I
decided to listen to all theories and hold my tongue and be
amused and keep my own counsel until I was convinced by
some concrete proof one way or the other.

Pat was a serious person. He was not afraid of ghosts nor
given to fits of insanity. He was what you might call a sound
man.

Like most sensible men Pat did not believe in faeries.

Then something occurred which changed his outlook. He told me what happened.

"One night I was returning from a visit to a good friend who was on his death-bed.

"I was coming down the road when I heard fierce crying behind the hedge. I went over to investigate. The moon was shining. Behind the hedge I saw a little white-haired woman. She was walking along the hedge but inside a large field.

"I walked along the road keeping my eye on her. She kept abreast of me the whole length of the field until she came to a high wall and barb-wire.

" 'This obstacle will put a stop to her gallivanting,' I said to myself.

"She went through the wall and barb-wire as if she were a tiger-tank!"

"I can tell you, Dano, I was astonished. Along we walked until she came to a deep stream. 'Now my girl you will have to jump or get your feet wet . . .'

"Again she crossed the stream as if she had walked on the water. That did it. I became afraid and sweat flowed down my brow. I made the sign of the cross and prayed to God for protection from this spirit . . .

"Do you think it was a faery you saw, Pat?"

"I am sure of it, Dano. It was the Banshee without doubt. She cried her head off while she was in my company but once I blessed myself and prayed she stopped crying and vanished," Pat replied with emphasis.

"That is remarkable," I replied.

"My friend died that night," Pat told me and added: "The Banshee knew he was going to die and was crying over his death."

"Maybe it was the devil disguised as a woman and crying because he was not going to get your friend's soul when the latter died next morning," I suggested piously.

"Could be?" Pat admitted reluctantly, "but I will still maintain that I saw and heard the Banshee . . . until the day I die."

Pat's story did not make me change my attitude.

CRAIG NA h-ALTAR

A knock came to the Old Man's door. "Who's there?" he asked in Gaelic.

"I'm Nicky Black," came the reply.

The Old Man got out of bed with difficulty. "What do you want?" he asked the young, handsome man at his door.

"I know you live alone and are growing feeble: Is there any thing I can do for you — like purchasing groceries, for instance?" Nicky Black wanted to know.

"Why should you offer to help me? I'm poor and not get ting any better tempered. Besides," the Old Man continued skeptically, "I never bothered to help elderly people myself when I was your age. I was a bit selfish. But I never did anyone harm either. Any harm I did in my day, I did it to myself."

"If you have no errant for me to run," said Nicky Black apologetically, "I'll run along and stop annoying you," and Nicky turned on his heel and began to walk off.

"I beg your pardon," the Old Man coaxed; "I'm crabbed these days with the pains in my joints, they have me driven demented, and it was good of you to offer help to an old man. Would you go to the shop and get me a bit of tobacco?"

Nicky Black came back to the door. "I'll be glad to oblige," he said with a smile. The Old man went in and rooted for coins in a trunk. He returned slowly to the door and handed over the price of the tobacco. "Righto, Nicky, I'm mad for a smoke; I did not have one in days. Don't be too long."

Nicky went off shopping and the Old Man returned to bed for a few minutes before getting dressed and settling down to carving wood. He was not many minutes working at his hobby when another knock came to his door. "Who's there?" he asked impatiently.

"It's Nicky Black," came the reply.

"He wasn't long," the Old Man muttered to himself as he stood up and straightened his back with an effort. He was getting more and more stooped. He scurred to the door, pulled back the bolt, and there was Nicky Black facing him with an out-stretched hand in which he held a plug of tobacco.

"I brought you a small cake for your tea," said Nicky lightly.

"A thousand thanks, Nicky Black," the Old Man said as he took possession of the tobacco and the cake. "It's years since I last tasted a fruit cake. God be good to you for helping an old man."

"Think nothing of it," Nicky Black said. "I'll be running off now. I shall call again next week, if I'm welcome?" Nicky pleasantly speculated.

"Oh, do come," said the Old Man gratefully. "I'm old and lonely. In spite of all, I like a chat, and anyways, if I'm still alive, I'll be looking for tobacco. The young may die, but the old must. You've heard that said, no doubt, Nicky? Ah sure it's great to be young and healthy. When I was your age I foolishly thought I would never die. But, when you get to my age and experience pains here, there, and everywhere, and get it hard to breathe, you realise it's a miracle your alive when you awake in the morning. Sure, it's making peace with my Maker I'll have to be doing?"

"Speaking of the Maker," said Nicky Black quickly. "I heard in the village that Mass will be celebrated tomorrow morning at Craig na h-Altar."

"Mass?" the Old Man said and his face lit up with pleasure. "Sure I'll be there if I'm to die in the attempt. "Will you be going there yourself, Nicky?"

"Alas, no," said Nicky regretfully. "I'll be helping some other old man then."

They said farewell, Nicky Black went about his business and the Old Man returned to his carving. But his mind was not on his hobby. His mind was full of contentment about the idea of a priest coming to the parish. There were few priests left in Ireland, he knew, since the coming of the Penal Laws, with their imprisonment, banishment, and killing of priests belonging to his Catholic religion.

It was a struggle but the Old Man felt in great spirits as he arrived at Craig na h-Altar before the priest and parishioners. After a wait like eternity, he heard voices and footsteps approaching. They came nearer. It was still a bit dark but the morning was dry and calm. Two men, dressed alike, crossed the ditch and went over to the Mass Rock. The Old Man had taken a seat under a bush near the streamlet, The Curiness, because he was suspicious; he did not entirely trust Nicky Black or anybody else, because it was still illegal to hear Mass, and the Protestant Yeomen were forever on the prowl for Catholic offenders.

One of the men opened a bag. He took from it a cloth, a book, a chalice, and two candles and some other articles and placed them here and there on the Mass Rock. The Old Man began to walk towards the priest and his attendant. "Pardon me?" he began with confidence, "which one of you is the priest?"

The two men looked startled. "My son," said one of them at last, "we are both priests, thanks be to God."

"Hear my confession," the Old Man ordered.

The priests spoke together in Latin before one of them walked some paces away from the Mass Rock and called the Old Man to him. In tears and terror, the Old Man made his confession — the first in thirty years. He felt weighed down by his sins. As he told them to Christ's apostle and received absolution, a lightness and joy filled his frail body and soul. Then he himself and the priest, whose name was Father John, went over to the Mass Rock, where the other priest, whose name was Father Bernard, stood robed and ready to begin Mass. The Old Man assisted prayerfully and received the Eucharist with every outward sign of devotion. Father John celebrated the second Mass, and the Old Man, despite a feeling of physical weariness, assisted at it too.

As the Old Man took his leave, the priests again conversed in Latin. Father John said: "We have just come off a French ship in Lough Swilly. Nobody in the diocese of Raphoe knew we were coming here today, except ourselves. How then, did you know we would be here this morning to celebrate Mass?"

The Old Man told the priests that he had been expecting but one priest, and that it was a young man by the name of Nicky Black who had given him the information.

"This Nicky Black must be a saint or an angel," said Father Bernard, "nobody in this parish had any news of our coming."

"There is one way of verifying whether Nicky Black is a saint or an angel," Father John said. He took a breviary from his pocket and began to read, and as he proceeded, the Old Man began to feel afraid. The priest stopped, and in an authoritative manner, said loudly: "You, Nicky Black, come forth."

No sooner said than the young man stood before the priests and the Old Man "In the name of God, who are you, and how did you know I would be here celebrating Holy Mass this morning?" said Father John sternly.

Nicky Black no longer looked young and handsome. In fact, as the Old Man watched in astonishment, he became transformed: He looked like half-man half-animal, his eyes, nostrils, and mouth gave off flames of fire and the air was filled with a horrific stench which emanated from his ugly form. He replied to the priest's question in the most ugly and despairing voice the Old Man ever heard. "I am Satan.'

The Old Man was unable to move or speak.

"Why did you tell this old man," Father John demanded, "that Mass would be celebrated here, when it is so pleasing to God and displeasing to yourself. Why, then, did you act charitably? – enemy of God and man!"

"I wanted to gain the old man's confidence, by running errands for him; by giving him correct information, even in religious matters; then, when he trusted me implicitly, I would lead him into sin, have him die in despair without the services of a priest, and torment him eternally in my kingdom of the damned."

A DANGEROUS JOKE

When I was nineteen I went visiting my Aunty Eileen in Sparrowstown one Sunday afternoon in September.

She was married to a man by the name of MacCadden. MacCadden was a farmer and cattle-dealer.

MacCadden's cousin, a chap by the name of MacCarry, who lived over the road, was sitting in my Aunty's kitchen drinking tea when I entered.

A relative of MacCadden's, by the name of Bennett, a wild lad, was living with my Aunty and her husband; he was born in America but liked Ireland and the Irish.

Apparently Bennett's family had sent him to Ireland to be reared and schooled, so that he would grow up far from the bad influence of the gangsters: it was the era of prohibition and depression in America. He was so wild and unruly his parents could not control him, and the police were busting into his home every turn round, questioning him about various robberies and street fights; and his family decided to send him to Ireland for a few years, to have him out of the way. . .

The three of us: Young MacCarry, Bennett and me played cards for an hour, and, when we got bored, we went down to Fortlough, a small lake below my Aunty's house. We strolled along the bank of the lake, throwing flags and little pebbles into its dark boggy water.

There was an old boat — bad cess to it any way! — lying on the bank. Says MacCarry to Bennett and me:

"We will put the boat on the lake and see if it will float?"

We managed to put it out onto the lake without much bother because we were strong, and the boat was small and light. The boat was six feet in width.

The boat floated but water came in through several holes; with the use of an old bucket, which we found lying beside the old boat, we bailed the water out as fast as it came in; we plugged most of the bigger holes with pieces of twigs and grass. Since there were no paddles or oars to be found near the old boat, Bennett made a suggestion:

"I guess, if we had a rope and tied it to the front of the boat, we could push the boat out on the lake; two of us could go on board while the third stays on the bank; when the boat has gone out on the lake as far as the rope will reach, the guy on the bank will pull the boat ashore; then he gets on board and one of the two in the boat takes his place on the bank, and pushes the boat out again onto the lake —"

"Dammit, that is a grand idea," I said. "That way we can get rides and pass the afternoon!"

"So it is," MacCarry agreed. "But where are we to find a rope?"

"I guess I can look after that chore," Bennett volunteered. And he ran up the path and heather to MacCadden's stables; and after ten minutes he returned carrying a halter which he tied to the stem of the boat.

"MacCarry and Bennett got into the boat. I pushed it out onto the lake according to plan. When it had reached the end of the rope, I pulled the boat ashore; they stepped onto the bank and we bailed out the water. MacCarry took his turn and I got into the boat, with Bennett; MacCarry repeated the performance; when Bennett's turn came, he pushed the boat out onto the lake — sensibly enough; but, by God, when we were out forty yards from the bank — the length of the halter, he shouted:

"Boys! I guess the temptation is too strong for me to resist!"

Without further ceremony Bennett threw the rope across the lake! There we were: drifting slowly away from the bank, towards the centre of the lake, where the water was over fifteen feet in depth! The bucket was on the bank!

Says I to MacCarry: "Do you see what the Yank has done?"

"I do," MacCarry replied. "The bastard means us to drown.

Bennett, you bloody bastard, wait till I get my hands on you
. . ."

Says I to MacCarry: "Keep cool! We must keep cool! Can
you swim?"

"Nay," said he regretfully. "I cannot swim, MacMahon."
Then he asked:

"Can you swim, MacMahon?"

I replied: "Not one stroke!"

That was God's truth. I could not swim in those days.

MacCarry looked at Bennett, who was standing on the
bank laughing, and shouted:

"Bennett, what did you do that for? You better do some
thing fast or we will get drowned!"

"What can I do?" Bennett asked sarcastically; he shrugged
his broad shoulders. "I cannot swim, I guess. Ha, ha, ha.
Swim for it, MacCarry; you long string-of-misery, dirty cheat,
card-trickster, old smelly feet . . ."

Looking back, I believe Bennett was mad! When he returned to America some years later, he lost his mind altogether
and was committed to an asylum. I am fairly sure he is still
confined in that institution.

The boat was filling with water.

"What are we going to do?" MacCarry says to me. He was
in despair.

"Apart from saying a good Act of Contrition," says I
cheerfully, "there is only one thing to do: that is to bail the
water out with the palms of our hands, since we do not have
the bucket!"

We tried, but we were not able to make much headway; we
could not keep the boat afloat and get it ashore at the same
time. If Bennett had gone off for help, we would have had
some hope, but he remained standing on the bank of the
lake, laughing his head off at our predicament.

We stopped bailing the water out and instead used our
hands as oars in trying to propel the boat forward.

I declare it worked! The boat quit drifting and gradually
moved towards the bank; and, after a bit of terrific scooping,
it ran for the shore. Still, the boat was not going fast enough
because the water was up to our thighs and we were afraid

the boat would sink before we got ashore. I coiled the rope, put a knot on the end of it, and threw the rope towards a clamp of bushes; the rope got caught very firmly between some branches, and I was able to pull the boat towards the shore.

By which time, the boat was practically filled with water.

"Get ready to jump, MacCarry!" I shouted. And as the boat sank, we jumped onto the bank, breathlessly. We lay down and rested.

When MacCarry got his wind back, he says to me:

"Only for your presence of mind, and sensible ideas, MacMahon, we could be out there in the lake getting our bellies full of bog-water!"

"We would be dead by now, I imagine," I said. "It is great to be still alive and able to relax, MacCarry!"

"Aye, it is. MacMahon, by your presence of mind and cool engineering you saved us from drowning," MacCarry said, gratefully. When he had recovered his wits, he looked across the bank to where Bennett stood looking in our direction.

MacCarry jumped abruptly to his feet, and said:

"I am going after that mad bastard of a Yank; if I catch up with him, I will kick the tar out of him."

MacCarry set off across the field in pursuit of Bennett.

They ran across many fields, heading for the high ground. When they disappeared on the other side of the nearest hillock, I returned to my Aunty's kitchen and told her what had transpired.

"You must forgive him because he is not all there! I do not know what we are going to do with him? He has been acting very strangely lately . . .!"

MacCarry returned half an hour later covered with sweat and looking vexed.

"Did you catch up with Bennett?" I asked.

"Nay," he replied.

"You must forgive Bennett, MacCarry, because he had not been himself recently," Aunty Eileen said apologetically.

"I have a confession to make," MacCarry said repentantly. He looked nervous and embarrassed. "I was at fault when Bennett played that joke on us: I had been cheating at cards . . .!"

DONKEY WORK

My brother Shea and I are quite unlikely to forget a rather discordant experience we had many years ago when we were adolescents.

In the Irish countryside, there used to grow — in great abundance, a wild berry, called 'The Blackberry Bush'. I suppose this simple name was given to the bush because its fruit was black, when ripe. In May, white blossoms appeared on the bush; by late July the blossoms were long since gone and had been replaced by a green knot, which, by the first week of August — depending on the weather — had turned red in colour, and, towards the end of August — again depending on the weather — the berry had become larger, and black — and ripe!

The fruit of the blackberry bush was mildly sweet in taste when consumed raw, and from it delicious jams and jellies could be made either in the home or factory. Mother often made jams and jellies and we never tired of eating blackberry jam and blackberry jelly.

After the war, jam manufacturers in Dublin and elsewhere used to appoint local merchants as agents, paying them a commission for buying, storing, and transporting blackberries and other fruits to their factories.

Since Shea and I were always on the alert for opportunities to make pocket-money, when the word spread rapidly across the parish to the effect that merchants in our villages were buying blackberries, at the rate of two shillings and six pence per stone, we volunteered. The response all round was fantastic: Quite like insurgents responding to a call to arms! —

little bands of workers, equipped with pots and pans and sundry containers of various shapes and sizes, were to be seen — here and there — behind fences, in woods, along public roads and lanes — picking blackberries feverishly.

It was difficult work despite the high spirits and the enthusiasm of most pickers, because the blackberry bush contained stabs and when we came into close contact with these stabs, we were scratched — some times on the face, legs, but most particularly — on the hand and forearm; and, when the scratch went deep, the pain was awful. Those stabs also tore our coats, stockings, shirts and pants. It was difficult work to be sure; some times we were surprised by an aggressive bull or ram; other times we were abused by eccentric farmers, who thought we were pulling down their gates and fences; that their cattle and sheep would thereby stray down the road or into their crops; many times we were forced to flee in haste, leaving our equipment and berries behind So, it was heavy going . . .

Shea and I gathered berries for two weeks without stopping. In all that time we only succeeded in filling a small barrel, because the bushes in our sector were not heavily laden with fruit owing to a heavy rainfall in the beginning of August. But, as you will see, this was only one of our minor problems. The really weighty problem was that of transportation: how were we going to get our fruit to the market?

"Uncle will give us the use of his little brown mare!" Shea said.

"No, he will not," said I; knowing uncle's ideas about the stupidity of adolescents, I was certain he would refuse.

"We will ask him," said Shea, hopefully running off directly to put the request to uncle. He returned, looking down cast. I knew, then, that we would have to eliminate the little mare from our list of alternatives.

"We could take a barrell on board the bus," Shea volunteered after some reflection.

"No," said I; "the conductor would not let us on board; you know how awkward public service transport workers are? We would have to pay for our own fares and in addition we might be charged for the barrel, because it is so big and would take up so much space on the bus; we would have nothing left for ourselves out of the money for the black berries —"

"We will have to think of something else besides the bus," Shea suggested. "Maybe Johnny Butty and his sister, Ann, might take our fruit?" Shea added.

"I do not think so," I replied. Johnny was insincere and unreliable.

"Why not?" Shea asked, surprised.

"Because, when they go to the village, next Saturday, with their fruit, they will have a very heavy load; they just would not take ours; their donkey could not carry two lots; no he could not." I told Shea frankly.

And so, we were now left with one possible alternative. I had a brilliant idea — and said:

"Oh! — we will get a lend of Parkers' donkey.' Mother, I remembered, had mentioned this possibility some days before, but we seemed to have given her suggestion no serious consideration at the time and forgot about it immediately.

"Aye, begod, that is what we will do " Shea shouted, impressed. He was delighted with the suggestion It was our last hope.

"We could give it a try," said I. Then I thought: 'What will we do if the Parkers are working with their donkey on Saturday'? Next I thought - and I spoke my thoughts aloud for Shea's benefit:

"There is the possibility the Parkers would not trust us with their donkey. Do you think they will?"

"That is the crack," Mother said, when we asked her opinion on the matter, later in the day. "You might meet with a refusal and that would be embarrassing . . ."

We withdrew for a private discussion. It would be embarrassing to be sure if we were refused but it would not be half so embarrassing as having to admit to our school-friends, and fellow-fruit pickers, that our fruit rotted in a barrel. This bleak possibility gave us sufficient initiative to approach the Parkers for the use of their donkey for an afternoon.

We reached a decision around noon on Saturday and an hour or two later we called upon our cousin Peggy Parker, and asked her, at point blank range, for the use of her donkey.

"Oh," Cousin Peggy said, good-naturedly, 'you are welcome to Jack any time!"

That is good news, I thought.

"The only thing, thought," Cousin Peggy continued: 'Jack is unshod and will have rough-going on the tarred roads.'

I said: "Let us see him." Jack was brought forward. He was a seedy specimen of an animal. He was small, grey-haired — more from age than nature, looked ill-fed and listless; in short, he made a very unfavourable impression on us all.

The market was located in the centre of a village six miles away. We thought it a convenient distance to transverse in a short harvest afternoon, but the serious error Shea and I made in our calculations concerned Jack. It became more obvious later in the campaign.

We started out at 3 o'clock in the afternoon and Jack seemed to have but two speeds — slow and stop! And, as we were going down the lane, Mother, standing in the doorway, having a look at our departure, shouted after us in a most en couraging manner:

"He will not make it," says she, meaning the donkey. "You will be lucky if he does not die on the way, either going or coming . . ."

We did not reply. We gave her the benefit of the doubt, that she was joking. We had gone four and a half miles when Jack stopped. Now, there is not anything odd in a donkey stopping for a rest, or, for any other perfectly normal reason — if he has a mind to do so; so long as he resumes the journey once he has had a breath of fresh air.

However, what we did consider a bit odd was the fact that he had halted going down an incline. It is normal for a horse or donkey to rest at the bottom or top of a hill, but not half-way down — going down hill!

Shea and I, in our casual careless manner, examined Jack's harness; it was fine. We sought for other annoying things, such as pins, or burrs, or faulty ropes, but, again, we met with a blank. What was the matter, then?

We tried diplomacy and coaxing and praise — no use! We then applied coercion, moderately, at first; but all to no avail: we had had to admit defeat. Jack simply refused to budge. Night was fast approaching and so, too, was quitting time in the market, and closing time for shops and other houses of business. We knew we would have to get a 'move on' or else return home forthwith — that is, if Jack were agreeable!

While Shea and I were thus engaged in a frustrating and helpless task, two elderly gentlemen came up the road. We were delighted to see them approach, because we were certain they would be willing to give us some help and sound advice.

"What is up, fellows?" one of the men said to me. Dan was his name.

"The donkey stopped about half an hour ago, for no apparent reason, and now he refuses to budge," Shea said, answering for me. Adding: "We have examined his harness but nothing is wrong with it."

"Could be the load is too heavy for him, lads," the second man suggested. His name was Michael.

"Nay," I replied; "because we have only a small barrel of blackberries in the cart!"

"That is funny," the two men said in unison, when they had looked over our cartage. They were experienced men — they knew all about horses and donkeys, we knew; but, to our horror, they, too, had to admit defeat! They went off perplexed.

The next person to come on the scene was a boy of about eighteen or nineteen years of age. Says he:

"The donkey is afraid of being run-over by his cart — look, chaps, at his feet, he has got no shoes on — no shoes on! No wonder, chaps, he has halted because he is afraid, that is why. There is only one good remedy, chaps: 'Take the cart off him and draw it along yourselves, otherwise you are going to be stuck here all night . . .' "

So, there we were, going down the road holding a shaft of the cart in our arms and Jack tied onto the tram!

We were making progress but Jack was pulling against us and we were still in a bit of a dilemma, because we were apprehensive about getting to market before closing time. We talked to each other — saying humorous things to lift our low spirits and we also prayed, hoping for a small miracle, and, to our immense relief, a little lady, of eight years of age, came down the road for a walk and picking blackberries as she came towards us. We asked her to do us a favour by leading Jack while we carried his load. She wondered at our strange predicament, I am sure, but she did not say so — this delicacy on her part suggested to us that she was in fact a lady.

Along went all four of us: Jack, the lady, Shea and me. A shopkeeper, by the name of John O'Galloway, saw us pass by his premises drawing the load which the donkey ought to be drawing. John came out of his shop, accompanied by a legion of boys, laughed, and asked us a mountain of questions of a teasing kind.

Looking back I feel positive that John did not help us out of any real sense of charity — but out of facetious curiosity. I appreciate that the scene must have appeared funny to almost everybody — ourselves excepted, of course. John and his companions escorted us into the centre of the village, which was a very kind deed for them to have done; and we thanked them profusedly and humbly. One remark, which I heard one of John's companions utter, concerning Jack's trouble in the cart, was:

"He'll britchen nane!" What the boy meant was: Jack would not attempt to hold back his cart while going down a hill.

I was told, later, that this chap used broad-Scotch freely.

The villagers had a hearty laugh at our expense and we were a bit embarrassed but we kept our true feelings under control and put on a 'could not care less' sort of front, thus fooling them all. However we were sensitive to the ridicule — the whole affair was humiliating and discouraging, because we had set out from home with hope, confidence, and a certain degree of self-sufficiency, and now — now, we were dependent upon a little girl to lead Jack into town and we ourselves were compelled to carry the fruit to market. It was all so very disappointing and discouraging . . .

Our entry into the village at this late hour was rewarded, however, because we managed to engage the attention of the merchants' purchasing officer before he retired for the day. He weighed our blackberries and wrote an entry in a ledger and handed us a duplicate copy of his entry.

"Take this docket up to Mr MacHughit!"

We proudly presented the docket to Mr MacHughit. He did not utter one word to us when we entered his shop. I noticed he was a gruff kind of fellow, fat, and smoked cigarettes.

"I am paying three shillings a stone for blackberries. I think it is a fair price. I hope you have not put water in the barrel to make the 'berries weigh heavier than they ought? — That would be cheating. You boys know that, don't you?" Mr MacHughit said severely, raising his heavy, dark eye-brows questioningly.

"By gosh, Mr MacHughit, we are sorry; I doubt we have thrown a splash of water over the blackberries to keep them fresh!"

I felt my face getting very hot and when I looked at Shea, his face had grown a ghostly pale. My pulse was racing —

"Ara, do not worry boys, I am sure you did the right thing," Mr MacHughit said kindly. He pulled the till out fiercely, gathered some silver into his fist and placed it in front of us: "Here boys," he said in a business-like manner, "is your money — eighteen shillings. Your blackberries weighed six stone — at three shillings per stone — that is eighteen shillings. Good luck, boys."

I took the money and moved across to the far side of the counter — away from Mr MacHughit. I was still emotionally upset. I knew my face was still flushed and that if I were to speak to him, I would be breathless, and Mr MacHughit might become violent, because he would know from my behaviour, and appearance, that I was guilty of fraud; we had not put the water on the berries to keep them fresh!

We bought biscuits to fortify ourselves for the return journey, chocolates for the little lady, presents for our brothers and sisters, tobacco for father, cigarettes for uncle, chocolates of a special kind for mother, and sweets for ourselves; we still had ten shillings left; and, cheered by our treasure, we set out on our return journey.

The sun was sinking behind the hills and we knew that darkness would soon be falling. Therefore, with vigour we journeyed homewards. This time Jack was between the shafts of the cart and when we reached the top of the long, steep hill outside the village, we got into the cart and urged Jack to greater speed, futilely. The journey seemed tedious, because night had fallen and we felt lonely as we stared at the stars twinkling in the sky. There was an uncomfortable chill in the air and altogether the whole business seemed to have been not worthwhile and we wished for home and our warm, cosy beds.

Out of the darkness a tall man appeared. It was father. Having been concerned at our delay, he had volunteered to meet us along the way. When he asked us what kept us so late, we explained the position as minutely as we knew how. It was a pitiful tale, and he drew a surprising conclusion, for he exclaimed:

"The old donkey has been taking a hand at you. To hell's gates with him, he is taking you for fools. He would not succeed in putting that joke across on me — I would have belted the arse off him!"

Father took a stick from under his coat and lashed out at Jack. Jack faltered for a moment. I suppose he did not know what was happening at first but it soon became apparent, for he leaped into high-gear — and no messing!

We had thought him incapable of such speed. We were quickly convinced of the validity of father's assertion. We were also convinced of Jack's treachery — he was giving proof of his perfidy before our eyes. Again we felt humiliated: we had thought ourselves tough but a little ignorant donkey was smarter than both of us.

Under the stimulus of blows and curses (of a saintly nature!) Jack covered the second half of the journey in a fraction of the time taken to cover the first part of it. Nevertheless we were famished with hunger and cold by the time we reached home, but mother had prepared supper before we arrived, and so we sat down, almost immediately to hot tea, buns, and blackberry jam. We gave Jack oats; perhaps, for him these were the first oats in months.

Shea and I suggested stabling Jack in one of our outhouses, for the night, with the intention of returning him to Cousin Peggy the following day — which was Sunday, by the way. But mother said:

"Tomorrow is the Sabbath. Return Jack to Peggy tonight. Jack has given you enough trouble already, so return him to his owner, tonight; we do not want him to die on our premises . . ."

We protested, but in vain. Mother insisted:

"That donkey is a proper nuisance; the sooner you deliver him to Peggy Parker the better for all concerned. It was a mistake getting him on the road to the market. A proper nuisance, I say. Get him home to where he belongs and never ask Peggy for a lend of him, again; do you hear? Never again, and that is final. All your hard work: picking the 'berries, getting them to market, and for what — a few miserly bob? Good Lord, will you never acquire sense . . .!"

We knew it was her final word on the subject, and honestly we did not give a damn any more because of our disgust with Jack. We took him back to Cousin Peggy, and thanked her — we thanked her most profusely because she had rendered us a unique service. And Cousin Peggy, happy to have been of service and obliging her relatives, said:

"Oh — it was nothing; you are welcome to Jack any time; any time at all . . ."

THE MISSING BICYCLE

Marty Den George is no longer with us, rest his soul. He was a fiery character; good worker, heavy drinker, incurable gambler, semi-cobler, match-maker, crofter, stonemason cum joiner and pseudo-politician.

It was said of Marty, that he would attempt to build a man-of-war ship — he was a very bold worker, possessing unlimited confidence in his artistic and creative genius. But, when he fell upon hard time, in his old age, he took to helping himself with other people's property.

Neighbours, who lost property, invariably believed Marty was the culprit; even when they recovered goods that they had mislaid, having blamed Marty for stealing these goods, they continued to regard him as a possessor of their property.

In all honesty, Marty was guilty of many, many thefts; since he did not always steal articles of use, modern psychology would regard him as being a kleptomaniac, for, in his will, he tried hard to make restitution, by leaving a sizeable sum for the repair of the local church of Glenmullan; however, he ungraciously added a codicile to his will, disclaiming responsibility for all the thefts that had taken place in the parish — adding, much to the annoyance of other addicts, that he was not the only thief operating in the parish.

It so chanced, that Marty took a bicycle from a parking lot outside Mrs O'Crowe's rambling house after darkness had fallen. The following morning he went into Drummulan, riding this new but illegally acquired mode of transport — and parked the bicycle outside MacCossingan's Inn; he went into the bar — ostensibly for a drink — and made inquiries where he could find a buyer for his bicycle.

Sergeant O'Lanagan was not more than two months in Drummullan at the time. He did not know many people, as yet, in his new precinct. All he knew about the neighbourhood was that it was a law abiding area; and he was determined to keep it that way while he was Sergeant of the local Gardai.

Marty learned from the talk of a Drummullanian, who was drinking in the Inn, that the Sergeant was looking around for a bicycle, and, with tremendous audacity, Marty went up to the Barracks and asked for an audience with Sergeant O'Lanagan.

The Sergeant came out to the hallway, to see his visitor, and was pleased to learn, that his visitor, instead of having a robbery to report, had a second-hand bicycle for sale.

"What is this, at all? Are you selling your bicycle? How much are you wanting for it?"

"See here, Sergeant," Marty explained, "my brother, Jackie, has up and gone off to work in Liverpool and will not be back home for at least five years. This is my bicycle. Because Jackie will not be using his machine until he returns, he said it would be all right for me to ride his old crock; so, once I heard you were looking for a bicycle, I says to myself: 'Marty MacCurtain', I says, 'sell your own bicycle to the Sergeant and send the proceeds to the foreign missions!' As sure as God is above in Heaven, that is what I said; now, would you believe that —".

"How much?" the Sergeant asked again with impatience.

"I thought I would sell it for half the money I paid for it over six months ago; if I do not send the money to the missions, I will buy a foal. Well, what do you think, Sergeant?"

"You have not told me how much you are asking for it," the Sergeant politely reminded Marty.

"Let me see now, let me see . . . now . . . I will . . .?"

Sergeant O'Lanagan examined the tyres, the brakes, the handlebars, the pump, the carrier, the tool-bag and the tools within, the chain and its cover, the saddle, and the three-speed-gear, and, before Marty could conclude his mental calculations, the Sergeant said:

"Not a bad bit of a bike! But the tyres are a stifle bit worn (the tyres were barely soiled, but the Sergeant had had to find some fault so that he could get Marty to reduce the price he was asking); regardless of this serious fault, how much are you asking for the bike?"

"When I bought it six months ago, I paid £16, with 10/- discount (the price its rightful owner had paid for it one year before, was £13; Marty knew this, but he said £16, so that he could lure the Sergeant into paying a higher price). I will tell you what, Sergeant? Seeing that it is yourself that is buying it, I will give it to you at a fair price, £8! — not a penny more or less . . . honest to God I would prefer taking it home rather than selling it for less than that, I declare to God! It is a good, and free wee machine, and, if I had it up for sale at an auction, I would be wanting £10; Jackie will be raging-mad with me for selling it for less, I declare to God! I will —"

"Could you drop a £1?" Sergeant requested hopefully.

"As sure as God is above us in Heaven, Sergeant, I could not drop the price by a penny, I am giving the machine away at £8!" Marty was emphatic and shook his head and sighed solemnly.

The Sergeant was convinced.

"You are an honest looking man; and I will be candid with you: I will give you eight pounds into your hand." He took a roll of currency from the breast-pocket of his tunic and rattled silver coins in his trouser-pocket.

Marty was interested and watched the Sergeant's movements closely.

Sergeant O'Lanagan started counting his money and said:

"I will expect a few shillings lucks' penny! Mr MacCurtain."

Marty shook his head wearily, sighed despondently, and said with obvious exasperation:

"By cripes, you drive a hard bargain, Sergeant; but, since your money might being me luck with the horse, I will give you the bicycle. Jackie will have my life for this . . ."

Actually, Marty could not have resisted a smaller sum if the Sergeant had known his failing: Once Marty saw the Sergeant's money, he would have sold the bicycle for whatever sum the Sergeant might care to offer. He gave the Sergeant five shillings lucks' penny, and said amiably:

"Care for a drink, Sergeant?"

The Sergeant disliked strong drink but graciously declined Marty's kind invitation, with:

"Maybe some other time!"

"I will be only too delighted," Marty assured the Sergeant and then he went home.

Three days later, when Sergeant O'Lanagan went into the Barracks by the front door, he noticed a tiny fellow standing in the hallway. One of his colleagues informed him that the tiny fellow wanted to see him, urgently.

"Send him into the office and tell him I will be along in a jiffy."

Five minutes later the Sergeant went into the office and sat down in a chair behind the low, long, rough counter. He looked the tiny fellow over sharply, and asked sternly:

"What can I do for you, my good man?"

The tiny fellow looked about him and appeared to have some considerable difficulty in putting forward his complaint.

When he spoke, he surprised the Sergeant with his fine, polished accent. Beginning with some pertinent remarks about the weather and the crops and the tourist trade, he finally came to the point:

"Sergeant," he stammered, 'I regret, most sincerely, the necessity of perturbing you with one of my problems: My bicycle has disappeared! I am of the opinion that it was stolen —"

"Holy Moses!" Sergeant O'Lanagan exclaimed with sympathy and surprise. "Has some bastard stolen your bicycle?"

The tiny fellow was startled and surprised at the Sergeant's crudeness.

"I am afraid so," he confirmed with gravity. He looked over the Sergeant's head at a photograph of General O'Duffy, leader of Ireland's pro-fascist Blue-Shirt organisation and former Commissioner of the Gardai, hanging on the wall behind the desk. The tiny fellow was a fanatical republican and socialist, who bore Eoin O'Duffy and his politics a great hatred, bordering on the pathological, but, on this showery morning, he had only one thought in mind – justice: the recovery of his bicycle and the punishment of the man who stole it!

"Let me have some details," Sergeant O'Lanagan requested in an officious manner.

"By all means, yes;" the tiny fellow replied with fervour; "what details would you like to have, Sergeant?"

"Well, for a start: What make was it?"

The Sergeant opened his notebook and licked the lead of his blunt pencil.

"The trademark was 'Robinhood'; I bought it last August –"

"A man's bicycle?"

"Yes, a gents – definitely," the tiny fellow clarified.

"And what is the serial number?"

The Sergeant was labouring over his notebook and spoke without looking up at the tiny fellow.

"My humble regrets, Sergeant; I cannot tell you that, I am afraid . . . perhaps Henry MacPaddock, who has the bicycle shop over in Sweetheart Street, might be obliging by letting me have a duplicate of the bill of sale; you see, Sergeant, I purchased my bicycle from Mr MacPaddock –"

"That would indeed be helpful," the Sergeant asserted with mock politeness. He disliked Henry MacPaddock ever since they met over a game of cards in the hotel.

"Any thing else?" the Sergeant wanted to know.

"It has a three-speed-gear, chaincover, pump, bell, carrier, and, quite recently I changed the tyres –

"It is a Robinhood, has a three-speed-gear . . ." the Sergeant repeated parrot-like, as he wrote the particulars of the stolen bicycle in his soiled note-book.

". . . It has wire-brakes, and . . . in fact, Sergeant, it is a ditto for the model you have standing in the hallway . . .!"

The tiny fellow thanked the Sergeant for his understanding and promise of help. He went directly to the bicycle shop in Sweetheart Street and asked Mr MacPaddock for a copy of the bill of sale and the serial number of his bicycle. Because he was too tight fisted to hire an expert book-keeper, Henry MacPaddock tried to keep his own records. He was an incompetent book-keeper and his records were always in a state of chaos, therefore he was unable to oblige the tiny fellow that time. The only thing he could provide was a general statement of account. Without the serial number it was almost impossible for the Gardai to recover the tiny fellow's bicycle; and for years Sergeant O'Lanagan kept searching and it right under his arse!

ANN MARIE'S EMBARRASSMENT

Ann Marie, a widow's second eldest daughter, was home on holiday from Scotland, where she worked as a cook in the home of the millionaire, Sir Malcolm FitzRobert.

Ann Marie visited her aunts and uncles before going to see next door neighbours and the relatives of Donegal acquaintances who worked with her or near her in Glasgow. She knew that if she returned to Glasgow without visiting the mother of the O'Rafter girls, they would verbally flay her to death. She knew also that if she did visit Mrs O'Rafter one of them would be asking:

"Where was Ann Marie going?"

And she would be answered by another: "To see what she could see with her sharp nose, the trooper."

The name of 'trooper' was the misnomer the O'Rafter girls used to describe a female whom they disliked for some reason or another, or for none. They became famous for insincerity and backbiting.

Ann Marie arrived at the O'Rafter house at 3 o'clock in the afternoon and wearing her newest dress. Mrs O'Rafter and her daughter, Rita, gave her a tremendous welcome. They sat down to hear her answers to their many questions about life in Scotland and about the health and doings there of the O'Rafter girls and others from Donegal. Time passed quickly. If they made her tea once, they made it for her half a dozen times. They made her feel that if she were an angel from heaven she could not have received a more affectionate welcome. For the moment she forgot her own mother's words when leaving home:

"Be careful what you tell the O'Rafters. They are as whitewashed as bedamned. Mind what I am telling you, Ann Marie. I know them. Their mother, Margaret Ann Murphy, who was only eighteen when she married forty-nine years old Den O'Rafter, came from a family of wealthy but ill-bred tailors. Every word you say in that house will be known at the far end of the parish before tomorrow night. So be very crafty, Ann Marie, give them no hint of your business if you are a wise girl . . ."

"Where is Kathleen today?" Ann Marie asked. Kathleen was the youngest of the O'Rafter girls. She was home on leave for a couple of months. In time, when her health had returned to normal with the change of air and the proper care, she intended to resume her work in a factory in Clyde Bank.

"Kathy has gone to Drummullan to do some shopping," replied Mrs O'Rafter. "She will be back in an hour or two. Wait until she returns for I know she will be delighted to see you, Ann Marie."

"How is she feeling — has she lost that dreadful cough she had when I last met her in Glasgow, Mrs O'Rafter?" Ann Marie, who was known for her kindness and sincerity, wanted to know.

"Sure the devil a thing is wrong with Kathy?" said Mrs O'Rafter with a twist of the lip. "She is over her little tout now. She is still the same Kathy. She will not let her piece of beef go with the dog."

"I am glad Kathy is well again," Ann Marie said with feeling. She knew that Kathy, despite all her faults and failings, had worked hard like her sisters and brothers to send her brother, Don, to Maynooth, where he became a priest.

"The O'Rafters were poor but virtuous. Almost every penny they earned was saved and forwarded to their mother, who paid Don's college fees at St. Eunan's in Letterkenny and then at St Patrick's in Maynooth.

Don was stout and short like his three brothers. He had studied industriously at the seminary but it took him an extra year to qualify in philosophy and theology because of his deficient educational background. To those outside his family Don appeared to be rather sore on money; not having earned it himself through sweat and blisters it was natural for him, neighbours said, to try to keep in step with the sons of rich men, in buying the latest and the best in sports gear and going on expensive and unnecessary trips abroad instead of taking summer jobs for the purpose of earning money for books and to pay for other minor — but to his family, crushing — expenses. No member of his family was ever heard criticising him on this account; on the contrary they were proud of the fact that one day he would be a priest and vastly superior in learning to any one else in their part of the parish. Until he was priested the girls worked and toiled and forgot about romance. By the time their prime task had been accomplished most of them were past marrying age according to convention; they were not particularly good-looking; and they were regarded as being cantankerous as a bag of weasels. None of the local bachelors would have one of the O'Rafter girls for a wife, saying:

"They are all as wicked as wildcats."

Ann Marie looked over the kitchen cum livingroom discreetly: It was neat, tidy and spotlessly clean. A few faded photographs of dead relatives hung on one of the walls; a photograph of Fr Don hung on the other, and was taken on the day he had graduated with a B.D. degree or on the day he was ordained to the deaconate. A more recent photograph of him, taken following the celebration of his first Mass, was said to hang in the front room; and that every time one of the O'Rafter girls passed it, she blessed herself.

Although Fr Don was administering to the faithful in Australia, his photographs filled the house with an aura of his sacred office. Even Ann Marie could feel it.

While her mother and sister were entertaining Ann Marie, and enjoying the news from Scotland, Kathy was coming over the road at a slow pace. The last quarter of a mile seemed to be the longest she had ever walked, and her load of shopping grew heavier with every step she took; her arms hurt, sweat ran down her face profusedly, and her temper, which was never good at the best of times, began to boil in righteous indignation at Rita's failure to meet her and help her the remainder of the way with her load of groceries, pots and pans, and other items purchased in Drummullan.

At last Kathy reached their lane. It was a calm day. She could hear Rita talking to her mother. Her indignation could not be contained one second longer, and so she broke out in foul language and words of recrimination against both women.

To verbally abuse one's mother, especially the mother of a priest, was considered outrageous by Mrs O'Rafter, who possessed an exaggerated sense of maternal dignity. For one of her daughters to abuse her in front of a stranger, was unforgivable. However, Rita and Mrs O'Rafter pretended they did not hear Kathy. But when she came to within a yard of the door and stood there cursing them to the pits for laziness and lack of consideration for her four and a half milk walk from town in the heat of summer and with a load of food and pots and pans, they braced themselves for action and dropped their pretence.

Kathy stopped shouting. Then a tin pot came flying over the half-door and bounced off the dresser. Astonished, Ann Marie sat half-way between the door and the fire wondering what would happen next. Another pot came flying, hit the floor, and bounced off the table; next, a frying pan bounced upon the floor and settled at the fire beside Mrs O'Rafter; finally, another tin pot hit the dresser and rolled here and there through the house. The noise was horrendous. Suddenly, there was a cease-fire, the bolt holding the door shut was pushed aside, and Kathy, perspiring profusedly and carrying two bags of groceries, entered the kitchen. When she saw that her mother and sister were entertaining a visitor she felt ashamed and could not bring herself to face Ann Marie because of her foul language and childish behaviour. She dropped the groceries and, whirling about like a top, ran into the front room and slammed the door shut with such force that lime fell off the wall.

Mrs O'Rafter and Rita, enraged because of the embarrassing situation in which they were placed by Kathy's outrageous behaviour in front of a stranger, uttered words of censure, ran after her with the apparent intention of giving her a piece of their mind and a trimming for her petulence.

Ann Marie felt embarrassed sitting alone in the kitchen while the fighting O'Rafters quarrelled like tinkers in the front room. Later, in spite of being pacific in temperament and refined in manner, she laughed to herself at the O'Rafter family's tift, but, on the other hand, she felt somewhat guilty.

"If I had stayed at home," she said to herself, "Rita would not have forgotten to meet Kathy, who has poor health, and none of this would have happened – at least they could not blame me for putting them to fight each other."

Ann Marie could hear oaths, vows, curses, threats as the battle continued in the front room; every now and then, as its owner was punched and pushed, a body hit against the door; although she could not hear Kathy calling her mother any vile names, she could distinctly hear Mrs O'Rafter shouting in religious astonishment.

"Imagine calling a priest's mother a whore; Jesus, Mary and Joseph! – imagine calling a priest's mother a whore . . ."

JOE MACMURRON AND THE FAIRY

When I was building a dwelling house for Art O'Callan near the village of Milford, an old man, by the name of Joseph MacMurron, passed by the site every day, between four and five in the afternoon. He named those walks his 'constitutionals'. He used to dander into the site on his way back and spend ten or fifteen minutes looking at our work and making various comments on the weather, architecture, and what not. When he got to know us he used to tell jokes and anecdotes to give us a laugh and help pass the time, and soon we were taking his visits as part of the day's routine.

One day, when Joe was resting on a heap of timber, the rain began to fall. He got to his feet and hurried into the site hut, where we joined him.

"Boys," says he emphatically, "the weather is broken. You will have these May showers for the next couple of weeks — until the new moon comes!"

"I am not delighted to hear you make that damp prediction," Martin O'Conal, our foreman-carpenters, said sadly.

"Maybe you are mistaken, Joe?" I said; "maybe we will have but a week of this drizzle."

Joe shook his head and spat on the floor. "I always know when it is going to rain," he began with conviction. "My eye gets watery — no pain though; but the tears gather there and run in torrents down my cheek. I could have told you a week ago about this long spell of wet, but I did not want to be bothering you. The girl-friend used to think I was sentimental, but the doctor told her that is the way my eye will behave until the day its mate closes, too." Joe laughed; and he spat again on the floor.

We sat in the hut for over two hours, hoping the rain would quit. O'Conal and the three labourers played cards. Joe and I talked about music, and, before we went home, he asked me to visit him some night for a tune on the fiddle.

"Who is Joe courting?" I asked one of the labourers who knew him.

"That is what he calls the wife," the labourer replied. "He calls her the girl-friend, never refers to her by any other name; he is an odd customer . . ."

As arranged, I arrived alone at Joe's place around 9 o'clock. The rain had stopped but the ground was sodden and a gale was blowing up. His wife met me at the door and bid me welcome.

She was not beautiful but comely and at least thirty years Joe's junior; she was tall and slender, dark haired and pale-faced; her eyes were hazel and her accent was 'up the country'.

Joe was sitting at the head of the table near the fireplace. He was glad to see me and after making some remarks about the night, lifted a case from the inside ledge of the kitchen-window, opened it gently, and took out a fiddle and bow. Artistically, he put resin on the bow and tuned the strings of the fiddle; taking it in his left hand and the bow in his right, he played a set of reels, finishing off with a set of gigs. He handed the instrument to me. I played the "Siege of Ennis" and the "Boys of Bluehill". When I returned the instrument, he made various comments on the tunes I played and on my style. He reached the instrument to his wife. I thought she would put it away, but no! – she played four tunes I had never heard before, and her playing was what you would call: professional. I was surprised. Joe explained:

"The girl-friend and I met at a Fheis fifteen years ago. We won prizes that day. Ah! – she was the best fiddler I ever heard, but, when she married MacMurron, she lost interest."

And, while we were talking thus, Mrs. MacMurron played a tune entitled "La Paloma" – a beautiful tune.

"What tune is that?" I asked. Mrs. MacMurron said:

"It is an old Italian tune, I think. It was the song the Emperor Maximilian requested before he fell: he was executed by a firing-squad belonging to Benito Quares, the President of Mexico."

"A very sad affair," I replied. I knew history fragmentally but I remembered this incident in the reign of Napoleon III. "Very sad," I repeated. So, that is the tune Maximilian wanted to hear before he died? No wonder, it is a lovely tune."

"Yes," Mrs. MacMurron said. "I like it; it was also the favourite tune of Maximilian's wife, Charlotte, Empress of Mexico."

Joe talked, and talked; his wife made supper. After supper Joe talked about the incident which cost him the sight of his eye. He was reluctant to talk about it. The whisky he drank loosened the tight grip he kept on himself.

"Many people," Joe began, "have asked, naturally, what happened my eye. To be truthful I often gave evasive answers, because I would have to spin them all a long, weird tale indeed, and 99% of them would think I was soft in the head, and not believe one word I would to saying. You may not believe me either when you have heard it. Do you believe in fairies, Dano?"

Joe watched me closely.

I did not know what to say because I had a feeling that he did believe in their existence.

"I am inclined to doubt their existence but I am still a young man and maybe before I am pension-age I will know one way or the other!"

"Frankly, Dano, you hold a contrary opinion, you being a learned young man but old Joe MacMurron believes in the fairies, and here is why:

"One night, shortly after I got married, while the girl-friend was visiting her mother, I was sitting over there at the table repairing a neck-collar for a horse when I heard a knock at the door. I was slow in answering, and what do you think? − a Wee Man − oh! − he was no higher than an eleven-year-old boy; he was dressed in fancy clothes: top hat and gold chain across his breast and he carried a cane. He stood there, smiling.

" 'Are you Joseph MacMurron, the fiddler?' His accent was Scottish. 'Could you oblige us tonight by playing music at a ball we are holding —'

" 'A ball?' says I. 'Where?'

" 'In a house out the Bakery Road,' I tried hard to remember seeing houses on the Bakery Road; there was only one house on that road, so I asked:

" 'In MacCloud's?'

" 'No, Mr. MacMurron,' says he, 'but in another house, closeby.'

" 'There is only one house I know of on the Bakery Road,' I told him, not convinced, 'and that is MacCloud's.' He did not make me an answer. Says I to him:

" 'Give me ten minutes to wash, shave, and change my shirt and shoes!'

" 'Go right ahead, Mr. MacMurron,' says he pleasantly; 'no hurry'.

"I put the fiddle-case under my arm and followed the Wee Man down the lane, across the Back Road and down the Bakery Road. He did not speak and neither did I. We walked down the Bakery Road, approximately four hundred yards, and, there in a field belonging to Andy MacCloud, was a tall house! A house my moustache — a castle! — a castle with a lovely avenue winding up to its portico; there were coaches parked on both sides. Says I to myself: 'Who could have built such a large mansion without my neighbours telling me of its construction?'

"I followed the Wee Man inside the castle. It had a lovely hall and as we went up this hall, I heard singing and laughter and witty chat coming from several rooms. He stopped at the door of one particular room and says he to me in a matter-of-fact sort of way: 'That is the ballroom, Mr. MacMurron. Come with me please'. He walked into the ballroom and stopped at a circular platform in the middle of it. There were two or three chairs on the platform.

" 'Mr. MacMurron,' says he, 'you can take a seat and tune your instrument, and I shall declare the ball open and announce the first dance of the evening when you have communicated your readiness to commence.'

"While I tuned the fiddle and put resin on the bow I looked around the room, at the furniture, walls, the lighting and especially at couples sitting along the walls. 'I will start with a waltz', I told the Wee Man and I gave the fiddle a few scrats. He nodded and said in an authoritative tone of voice, the kind you would hear a flunkey use in one of those big hotels in Dublin or Glasgow:

" 'Ladies and gentlemen, the ball is commencing; please take your partners for the first dance of the evening. It is a waltz. Thank you'.

"I played different kinds of tunes: sets, lancers, gigs, reels; and they danced them all perfectly. And never in my life did I watch better dancers but what really set me thinking, was the fact that I did not ken one couple. I thought it strange to tell you the truth. They were a merry crowd – they danced, shouted, sang and cheered.

"The Wee Man would come over to me every hour and hand me a drink of wine mostly. Great stuff. Never tasted the like of it before – never. Supper was announced. The dancers left the room and in comes a gang of page-boys, dressed in green and red uniforms, with yellow braids; they set tables in rows, and covered the tables with snow-white cloths; set places with lovely china pieces and sparkling glass-ware. Then they carried in turkeys, ham, chickens, ducks, vegetables, fruits, water, and the devil knows what. All the time the Wee Man shouted directions and when the tables were set and the food placed along the centre of those tables, he called out: 'Supper is ready'. The couples trooped into the room again and took their places at the tables in an orderly manner; I too, sat in as directed by the Wee Man.

"The ladies were dressed lovely and wore precious jewels; the men wore striped-trousers and swallow-tailed coats."

Joe's wife put turf on the fire and Joe advised me pull my chair closer to the fire, and continued:

"Supper over, I played a set of slow tunes and the couples danced as gaily as before; the ball broke up at four in the morning. The Wee Man led me into a room at the far end of the hall and asked me to name my fee. I said: 'Thirty Bob (shillings)'. The Wee Man pulled out a drawer and gave me a five pound note. Well, I was more than pleased with my night's wages and he walked out with me as far as the Bakery Road. I was going to put a number of questions to him about the castle and himself, but, before I could square myself to ask them, he said gravely:

" 'Mr. MacMurron. If you ever see one of us again — in Milford or elsewhere else, I charge you most solemnly for your own good, not to speak to us; just walk by; do not take any notice of us; do not, I repeat, do not dally, tend to your own business and ignore us entirely'."

Joe stopped, spat into the fire and turned to me: "Would you believe what I am going to tell you, Dano, that that was the gist of what the Wee Man said? Mind you, I did not think his request at all strange, because, it was the custom, years ago, when the old gentry were here, to keep to yourself, until they made the first move.

"The Wee Man thanked me again and wished me a safe journey home; when I bid him good night I looked back towards the castle: it was in its glory, the avenue glittered, bright lights shone forth from many rows of large windows, and I marvelled that such a mansion could have been built on the outskirts of my small village without it being the talk of the neighbourhood. What they heard, I heard; you know how it is in a closed neighbourhood?"

I said I did! Joe went on:

"I turned for home, wondering as I went along; I was so full of curiosity that I looked back at the castle, but it had vanished. It was gone, I declare! The lights had gone out but the dawn was well up and if there had been a castle there I would have seen it; yet, all I could see, where the castle had stood, was a big rock — a rock we used to play on long ago when we were children going to school.

"When I awoke late the next afternoon I thought I had been dreaming. But I could not put the pictures of the night out of my mind — no dream could be so vivid, so real, I knew. The five pound note also was real. It was in one of the pockets of my Sunday suit. After I drank a cup of tea and swallowed a piece of bread, I set off down Bakery Road on the bicycle to investigate. Not even a cart-track could I detect near the big rock in MacCloud's field or in other fields nearby. On my way home I went into Barrett MacSpake's public-house to make discreet inquiries — but damn the word of a ball did I hear that day or since. I made further inquiries regarding house-building in the area, but dammit, not one person could tell me any thing about buildings of an unusual nature . . .

"So I held my tongue – not saying as much as one word concerning my experience; I dismissed the whole thing as a dream or hallucination or whatever else it might have been – I am not a learned man. I tried to find an explanation for the fiver (£5), but could not find one."

Joe took another sup of whisky and asked me if I would have another glass of lemonade; then he went on with his story:

"Years passed before I spotted any one who was at the ball and I wish to God I had never laid my eyes upon one of their kind again. It was a May-fair-Day in Milford. I was walking down Main Street when I met the same Wee Man coming up towards the cow-market. He was dressed in riding boots and britches, and carried a little cane, as well as wearing the tall hat and swallow-tailed coat. I was meeting him directly on the side-walk. Says I to myself: 'If I walk past without speaking, he will think I am odd'!"

Joe took another sip of whisky and spoke sadly:

"I looked sharply at him as he approached. 'It is he?', I says to myself; I was not quite certain, because, as he came nearer, I hesitated. And, then I says to myself: 'If it is your old acquaintance and you pass him by without speaking, he might be offended'; when we came abreast I stood, and said: 'How are you doing? I am very glad to meet you again after all these years'. He stopped, looked surprised – not kenning me. 'It is a long time since I played the fiddle for you at the ball! I am Joe MacMurron, the fiddler!' I reached my hand to shake hands; but he did not respond. Says he to me: 'You have mistaken me for some one else! However, since you see me, Joe, please tell me, with which eye do you see me?'

"Sure I thought he was codding, or had too much to drink! 'What eye, indeed? I see you with both eyes, surely'!

" 'No, Joe, you saw me with one eye only; which one is it, I would like to know'.

" 'What do you mean?', says I getting a bit annoyed.

" 'Put your hand over your right eye, Joe, and test if you can see me with your left eye?'

" 'Nay', I said, 'I cannot see you with my left eye, sure

enough!' That was strange, I thought.

" 'Now', says he, 'cover your left eye'.

"I covered my left eye. 'I can see you again', I told him. With that: He made a prod at my right eye with his cane and before I could step aside or cover my eye with my hand, he jerked forward with his hand and hit my right eye with the point of his cane. I felt a slight pain and a trickle of blood rolling down my cheek. I could not see the Wee Man any longer. The sight was gone out of my eye, for ever!"

"Great Scott!" I said; "Joe, that is the strangest story I have ever heard. Is it true?"

Joe sighed. "It is the truth!" he replied.

"Amazing!" I said.

Joe took another sip of whisky, and said:

"Because of the fairies I have been blind in my right eye for the past fifteen years . . ."

THE MAD WIDOW

The widow O'Mahony had two daughters, who were taller than herself. She was a tidy piece of fluff when a teenager. However she was bandy legged and her hair was red.

Before she married, the widow was to be seen at fairs, dances, sports and regattas; because she was often competing in sporting events, she was considered wild and reckless.

While she was still a slip of a girl she married Rory O'Mahony, who was over forty. She was seventeen at the time of her marriage.

After sixteen years of marriage Rory O'Mahony died suddenly and was buried with his own people in Innisowen.

A fellow by the name of MacHanrahan, who lived on a farm next door, used to go over to visit the widow and her daughters from time to time and give them a helping hand with the crops and herds. He was seven years younger than the widow but almost twice the age of her eldest child. This daughter was beautiful; and word got around the district that he fancied the daughter but trifled with the widow's affections while waiting for the daughter to become of age. Whether there was an element of truth in these stories, no one can now say for sure. In any event when MacHanrahan and the widow were courting in the barn one night, he got carried away and ups and asks her, there and then, would she come over to the chapel in the morning with him to have the priest tie the knot for the two of them in wedlock. She said she would.

MacHanrahan did not accompany her to the chapel as planned; instead he is supposed to have told her he had changed his mind, that his mother would not agree to the match, that he had not enough money saved, that he was not old enough. It was the case of the willing bride and the reluctant groom!

The widow had had to return home without another husband in tow. Like any normal woman, she was furious; but for her daughters' sake she kept her vexation under control for the remainder of the day.

When the Massfolk were coming home from the chapel the following Sunday morning, MacHanrahan — accompanied by his pals, while passing a group of women, which included the widow — made some wise-crack and the widow thought he had made it at her expense. Then she flared up at his sarcastic remarks, and shouted stoutly:

"Argus MacHanrahan, you will not be laughing and taunting at me this day week!"

And neither he was! He was underboard by that time the following day week!"

Apparently MacHanrahan was driving cattle up an old mountain path at the bottom of Slieve Dubh when she approached him carrying her late husband's old shot-gun. She gave MacHanrahan the contents of both barrels — at point blank range — by all accounts. He had thought she was out shooting crows and he passed no particular heed of her until she aimed the gun at his belly. Then it was too late. He panicked and made a dash for safety; she fired at him as he ran for cover at an old gate, hitting him in the lower part of the back, and arse, while the Angelus Bell was ringing down in Macamishmore.

MacHanrahan lingered on for an hour after being hit, and a crowd gathered. The shots were heard far and wide and people, seeing what had happened, sent messages to the priest, the doctor, and the Guards. MacHanrahan was still conscious when the priest arrived, but when he tried to get close to the dying man, to administer the last rites of the Church, the widow barred his way; the priest spoke calmly, and kindly, and succeeded in pacifying her for the moment.

Widow O'Mahony went home after the priest told her MacHanrahan was dead. She packed some food and a box of cartridges into a shooting-bag, slung the shot-gun under her arm and walked down to the bay, where her late husband's old boat was anchored. She waded out to the boat and climbed on board.

O'Mahony used to fish lobster and she used to do the rowing for him. When the guards arrived, and stood on rocks and cliffs overlooking the bay, she rowed the boat out further and dropped anchor.

Many people used to feel sorry for her when she married a man thirty years her senior but the fact of the matter was: She worked the poor man off the face of the earth. He was a saucy type of customer when he was young — would not dip his fingers; but when he married her, and she had got control of his life and farm, she put him out to work in all sorts of weather; he worked on roads, in stone quarries, on oil tankers in the bay, digging drains, cutting turf on the mountain, fishing the four seasons of the year. She helped him at the fishing and on the farm — give her her due. But she went far too far. When he was laid out many people thought he was the happiest-looking corpse they had ever seen . . .

As soon as the Guards arrived from Drummullan, she fired at them, and they ran for cover. Then, more Guards arrived from Letterglinchey and Manor-MacHarter. These late-comers laughed at the idea of the Drummullan Guards being unable to arrest a crazy woman, with nothing more lethal than an old shot-gun. But, by evening-fall, they knew what a difficult task they had to perform: she wounded three of them; that piece of misfortune put the laughter to one side. She sat at the helm of the boat when they fired at her; then, she would creep up the bottom of the boat and fire over the gib and retire to the helm; when they returned her fire, she raised the gib of the boat in a rocking movement, letting their bullets hit the side of the boat.

An old soldier, standing beside the sergeant who was directing operations, said:

"Look at that . . . that is classic. By jove she is a professional! I never saw the like of that . . . Look! Look! . . . I . . . could not do better myself, take my word for it . . ."

The Guards sent a message by telephone to the military in Dun MacCool, which was on the opposite side of the bay, requesting help. The army sent out a gunboat to attack her from the rear and to prevent her from making her escape by sea. She moved out further in the bay to meet the challenge from the gunboat. She fired at it until she ran out of ammunition.

Meanwhile the priest arrived. For a few minutes he stook watching the gunboat, the Guards, and the widow, shooting it out for death and life. He was very annoyed. He blessed himself and opened a prayer book and began reciting prayers. As he proceeded to recite prayers, perspiration ran down his face and reek began to rise out of his grey hair.

When the priest had finished reading, and praying, he shouted:

'Thanks be to God. Thanks be to God: I have saved her soul!' Then he fell on the grass, exhausted.

Someone standing near said: "Are you all right, Father?"

"Grand. But I am jaded after my struggle with Satan and his evil forces!" The priest revealed later what he meant by those words: "When she ran out of ammunition, and knew she would be captured, a demon swam beside her boat, inviting her into the water, and advising her to drown herself rather than let herself be arrested. As I prayed, the demon swam away, leaving her in peace, because he had not succeeded in enticing her to take her own life. Satan wanted her soul but I beat him this time, thank God!'

Widow O'Mahony seeing the army gun-boat approaching, and not wanting to put her virtue at risk by surrendering to soldiers, rowed her boat towards the shore and allowed the Guards to take her into custody.

FAMINE

I stood in the heather beside the Corby Rock and watched the people. They looked sad and emaciated in their ragged clothes. My eyes viewed the faces from the front row to the endless tail of the procession. They seemed familiar yet I knew nobody personally. But an inward voice told me that they were all related to me ancestorially. However, since I did not know them personally I could have no sympathy with their cause, whatever it was. If they were materially, politically, or religiously repressed, I was indifferent to their plight because I felt no emotion.

"There is a famine in the land," one of them told me.

"A famine?" I said. Perhaps there is a famine because you are all beggars instead of workers. You have not worked, you will not work, and you do not intend to work."

The people's squalor began to sicken me. They reminded me unpleasantly of unwashed and low-classed tinker women whom I saw from time to time visiting my home when I was a child. Why were they reliant upon an inept government for subsistance instead of being self-supporting? Were they not too lazy, too indifferent to educational opportunities, and too stupid to promote their material and religious well-being? Then I seemed to lose my contempt until I again felt no emotion whatsoever.

I scanned the procession from front to the turn of the road. I let my eyes come back to the front of the procession before I moved a step or two towards the road. It was then that I identified one of the women: She was my maternal Granny. She walked in the front row. I shouted:

"Where are you going, Granny?"

She stopped walking, and with her stopping the whole procession came to a sudden and complete halt. It was then that I noticed the men in the procession. I put the question to Granny again before she answered:

"We are starving of hunger," she said sadly and faintly. We are walking to Milford for food. We have heard that the authorities are distributing grain at the Workhouse."

The Corby Rock, before the County Council blasted part of it away in order to widen the road between Kerrykeel and the Milford Bakery, hung frightenly over a part of the roadway.

The day was sunny with the smells of Summer blowing in the breeze. It was approaching harvest time.

"The potatoes have entirely failed because of blight," Granny told me sorrowfully. "There is nothing to eat. The oats and cattle have been sold to pay the rent. Now we have nothing left for planting. What is going to become of us?"

As I listened, my heart began to grow sad for these people and I felt that the hand of God was upon the world. I stood aside helplessly. I did not remember replying to Granny's question before she continued:

"Join with us in our procession to the Workhouse for food. Many have died and many more are at the point of death and many others will die if God does not send food through the charity of other countries because we have very little money of our own. Pray, pray, pray." When she had finished speaking she walked off leading the procession. I climbed above the Rock to get a better view of the people marching past. I heard their voices raised in prayer. I asked myself?

"Sure my friends are living on the other side of Milford, out the Termon-Kilmacrennon way; it does seem strange that Granny and her blood relations are walking towards Milford from the Fanad side. Besides, did not Granny die in 1952?

What is she doing leading a procession in search of food to Milford Workhouse when she is dead, the Workhouse is a ruin, and her ancestors live in the district of Kilmacrennon? Furthermore, sure the Great Famine occurred well over a hundred years ago?

I awoke. My dream remained with me the whole day because of its vividity. I had not been reading of the Great Famine of late, and why was my Granny the main character? I reflected. Granny had told me many stories about the Great and other latter Famines. She had also taught me Christian doctrine. Perhaps my dream was nocturnal viewing of childhood stories?

When searching for a document amongst a pile of papers I saw again Father Shouriah's letter telling me about famine-stricken India. Then I knew why I dreamt the night before about the Great Famine in Ireland and about my Granny.

I re-read Father Shouriah's letter. It told me of the plight of his humble people who were living on the verge of starvation because of droughts, floods, and typhoons. But the first reading must have made a lasting impression even though I had taken no action by way of response to his appeal for help.

"In our selfishness," someone wrote, "we are more concerned with a tootache than with an earthquake in Peru which has killed hundreds and left thousands injured, homeless, and starving." I threw the letters aside, cleared my desk, took out my typewriter, and began to draft a letter of appeal to editors. Here are two of the anecdotes I incorporated in my letter of appeal for funds:

"There is a townland in Donegal called Drumhallagh Lower. In this area only one potato field escaped with a relatively mild attack of fungus blight. It gave its owner a little below average yield. He was reasonably satisfied with his crop of potatoes; but to his less fortunate neighbours, whose potatoes had failed entirely, his field seemed to have given him a bumper crop; and, after he had dug and stored away his potatoes, they gathered from miles around and re-dug his field seven times in the hope of finding more potatoes.

"In a neighbouring part of the County another man,

whose potato crop had failed entirely, was rather fortunate in a field of turnips with which to feed his large family. His wife used to cook the turnips in a big iron pot. His family seemed to be managing fine on this restricted diet until one day the bailiff, at the command of their landlord, came to collect the rent; the man with the field of turnips was so poor in other respects that he did not have sufficient money to pay all of the rent due, and the bailiff, who was also a poor, and a sympathetic person, acting on the landlord's instructions, to make up the balance of the rent, took the only appropriate piece of property he could find on the poor man's farm, the iron pot. From that day forward the man's family was compelled to eat raw turnip."

MARRIAGES ARE MADE IN HEAVEN

The new Bishop of Raphoe paid visits to schools, convents, factories, public offices, hospitals and so on soon after his consecration.

The last hospital on his list was that of St. Conal's, the County's mental hospital. Today it is referred to as the psychiatric hospital.

The new Bishop was shown from ward to ward by the head psychiatrist, Dr. O'H-----.

A nurse came running down the corridor shouting: "Doctor, Dr. O'H-----, you are wanted on the telephone."

Dr. O'H----- excused himself and told the new Bishop to wait a few minutes.

While the new Bishop was awaiting the return of Dr. O'H---- he strolled up and down reading his breviary. He was thus engaged when a patient came round the corner and collided with him.

"O, I am sorry, my son," said the new Bishop by way of apology.

"Forget it, brother," said the patient jovially, sure I was in too much of a hurry and was not watching where I was going. I am plain busy. They have me working like a Trojan since I was permitted to leave my cell. I am now quite all right, sane at last. Would you believe it?" He looked the new Bishop over suspiciously. "What is your name and what has you here in this madhouse," he asked sympathetically. Adding: "There are some hard cases here," and he pointed to the cells on both sides of the corridor.

"Actually," the new Bishop began to explain faintly smiling," I am just paying a pastoral visit to this hospital. Reaching his hand to the patient he added: "My name is Dr. MacN-----, the new Bishop of Raphoe.

The patient drew closer and looked the new Bishop over very carefully after shaking his hand. Then he shook his head, looked about him to make sure no one was listening, and said kindly in a lower tone:

"Ah, do not worry about being the new Bishop of Raphoe. In here all members of the medical staff really know their business and will have you as right as before in no time unless you are gone too far; you look all right to me; they will soon put that notion of being the new Bishop of Raphoe out of your head — when I came in here two weeks ago I thought I was the new President of Ireland." He patted the new Bishop's shoulder compassionately and walked up the corridor leaving the new Bishop standing rather perplexed.

The next minute Dr. O'H----- returned and apologised for his delay. The new Bishop understood the pressures of medicine and said: "I trust I did not rush you, Doctor?"

After resuming their stroll through the hospital, they entered a cell where the patient was sitting on a stool holding his head in his hands and looking at the floor. He answered the head psychiatrist's "Good day, Harold", with a mutter. The new Bishop spoke words of consolation but the patient did not as much as mutter.

Out in the corridor the new Bishop asked Dr. O'H---- the name and cause of Harold's illness.

"As far as we can ascertain," Dr. O'H----- · began to explain, "Harold was in good health until his fiancee refused to marry him at the last minute.

"O, the poor fellow," the new Bishop said compassionately, "Poor man, if only he knew it was for the best I am sure; after all, marriages are made in heaven. This he ought to have understood, and accepted the will of God. The girl was meant for some one else perhaps and this was why she refused to marry Harold. Besides, he should have turned to St. Raphael for help."

"Why St. Raphael?" Dr. O'H----- asked pleasantly. "What could Raphael do for him?"

"Do you remember the biblical story of Tobias and Sarah, how the Archangel was sent by the Lord to cure Tobias' father, Tobit, of blindness and to drive away the demon who was killing Sarah's husbands?" asked the new Bishop.

"Now I recall the story!" Dr. O'H----- exclaimed with interest. "I recall the medical aspects of the story, certainly."

They entered other cells until finally they came to a cell at the far end of the corridor. It had padded walls and the floor was covered with canvas. Great shouting was coming from the cell. At the door the Doctor, instead of opening it, pulled across a slide and looked through the peephole.

"Eustace is really violent today, Dr. MacN-----. Look for yourself".

The new Bishop looked through the peephole. "O my gracious, Dr. O'H-----," he exclaimed, shocked. "This poor man is very ill. What has made him so violent?"

The patient was running back and forth, throwing himself forcefully against the wall and onto the floor, where he would lie screaming, frothing at the mouth, and kicking like a horse in the last throngs of a painful zoological disease.

"Eustace," Dr. O'H----- said, resuming his place at the peephole, "suffers from hysteria. During attacks he would be inclined to sustain a grievious injury but for the padding which prevents him from knocking his brains out.

"Poor man", the new Bishop said again. "What caused him to become so violent."

"I gather," Dr. O'H----- began to explain, "that Eustace's marriage was far from blissful. His wife, who is a spendthrift and a snob, constantly nagged him about his low income. He was pressurised into working longer hours in the factory and in the kitchen when he came home in the evenings. He often came home to an empty and untidy home. As often, she would be drinking and playing golf with other social climbers; whereas Eustace was the quiet, gentle type. Through her socialising, neglect of her home, and nagging she made a major contribution to bring on Eustaces insanity. He will never be the same again. Harold," Dr. O'H----- explained, "will revert to type."

"Which is?" asked the new Bishop.

"An extrovert," replied Dr. O'H-----. "But for Eustace we cannot do very much, I am afraid. Yet," Dr. O'H----- speculated, "no one is entirely without hope. We can always ask for the prayers of the clergy," he continued with a smile, "I invite you to pray for Harold and Eustace because they have one thing in common."

"What is that?" the new Bishop asked with interest.

"The same woman drove both of them insane.

The new Bishop was incredulous: "Do you really mean to say that the wife of Eustace was the woman who had refused to marry Harold at the last minute?"

"I meant that precisely," Dr. O'H----- confirmed before shutting the slide and walking down the corridor in the direction of the staff canteen.

SNOBBERY

When Gregory MacGarvey came home from hospital an old cohort, Dermot Bane O'Tool, paid him a courtesy visit.

"How are you feeling, Gregory?" Dermot Bane asked concernedly when he saw his friend's haggard face.

"God and His Blessed Mother, and all His Holy Saints above in Heaven, be praised; I cannot say a word of complaint."

"That is well said," Dermot Bane asserted. "We must be resigned to the will of God; so the Mrs keeps telling me when cattle and sheep die, or, when any thing else of that sort goes wrong; the Mrs is a great woman for trusting in and accepting the will of God!"

"I will live another couple of years with a little bit of care and encouragement," Gregory said, wanting his friend to pay close attention to his pronounciations. He shrugged his bottle-shaped shoulders and laughed a very nervous laugh. He wanted to be gay, to be brave about his illness which he knew was fatal; to convince others — as much as himself — that he was in good health and might live another five years, at least. "They say it is very hard to kill a bad thing! Weeds are hard to keep down!"

"What was it like in hospital, Gregory?" Dermot Bane was anxious to know.

"Man dear you would think you were in a hotel in Bundoran; the food was very good and there was plenty of it, too. The nurses could not do enough for you; and the matron took a fancy to me, as God would have it. I was humming a piece of *The Hills of Donegal* one morning when I was feeling lively and frisky; she was passing the ward and hearing my song, she comes in and stands at the foot of my bed; says she to me:

"'Are you a ballad-singer, Mr MacGarvey?' Dammit, Dermot Bane, I had to laugh!"

"Of course you had surely. It is great to be able to charm the women with a verse of a song. In olden times, the women preferred men with good singing voices, I believe!" Dermot Bane said historically.

"I suppose they did, but not in my young days. However the wardsmaids were pleasant, too. There was one wardsmaid there, a fine thing, about twenty-eight, but a bit on the plum side, unfortunately, who, when polishing and cleaning, used to lean over the table and bend down at the window-ledges and skirting-boards — and my God —"

"I know!" Dermot Bane said understandingly. "She would give you impure thoughts and a new lease of life!"

Gregory raised his eyes skywards, let out a sigh of controlled passion, and interposed with:

"To encourage a virile fellow to co-operate with her in giving some non-existent person an entirely new lease of life would be more to the point, if you know what I mean? But seriously though, the girls nowadays wear their skirts far, far, too short. It is a disgraceful habit: they appear to have no shame. I do not know how the young men remain pure —"

"Sure what is the use of talking? I am always lecturing my girls because they disgrace me; and they should be ashamed of themselves for going around with their skirts level with their arses! 'All I see', I keep telling them, 'is: arses, and more arses'! I do not know what the world is coming to at all. God will put a curse upon the world if we are not careful and pray harder and put more pressure on the young people to behave in a decent manner. The Mrs is always on to Mary and Bridget for wearing short skirts, but, sure she might get better results if she went up to the tip-top of Knockalla and shouted accusations at the soldiers in Dun Ri Fort!"

"The next thing you will see, Dermot Bane, is your daughters and their friends wearing skirts as short as their elbows!"

Gregory laughed but his laughter was not as nervous as it was before. Dermot Bane shook his head despondently, and pronounced frankly:

"It is hateful for a father to be confessing that he cannot get his daughters to dress decently —"

"Maybe God will send us back the ice age; that would force the ladies to cover what God gave them to cover. Oh! Woman would risk getting pneumonia by wearing nothing on a frosty morning if she thought she would get the finest man in town to have notions of she!" Gregory asserted with half-hearted conviction.

Dermot Bane, remembering that Gregory was supposed to have begotten an illegitimate daughter when he was a servant boy in County Tyrone, five and forty years before, grew flushed.

Gregory felt a little dizzy and his guts rattled like distant thunder.

For a three minute period the two old cohorts were silent. They looked into the fire and watched the flames shooting up and coils of grey-gassy smoke shooting out of the English coal.

"You went through a dangerous operation?" Dermot Bane asked casually although hoping to learn exactly how many operations his friend had undergone. He knew that his wife would be asking questions about Gregory's illness, and would be disappointed if he could not give her a complete and detailed report when he went home.

"Six!" Gregory boasted.

A Donegal man hates being ill, and will use any and every strategem to convince himself, and his friends, that he is not ill; but once he is certified, and has been admitted to hospital, and his illness is at last publicly acknowledged and acclaimed, he will resign himself to his fate and magnify his sufferings when relating details of his illness to friends and acquaintances. By doing so he thinks he becomes a hero instead of a weakling!

"Who was the butcher?" Dermot Bane asked flippantly, trying to reduce his friend's experience from the extraordinary to the common.

"A good man, I am told; one of them black surgeons, an African bucko. He is the silent type, but very good with the knife, and, to think, three years ago them buckoes were killing Irish soldiers in the Congo!"

"I think you are wrong, there," Dermot Bane corrected Gregory. "It was not the Blacks, but the Balubas who killed them. The Blacks are a decent lot of men. The Balubas are a dangerous crowd — savages, worse by far than the Orangemen of old!"

"Blacks are taking over in this country; in the next century Irish men will be black instead of white men!" Gregory forecasted with gloom.

"It goes to show you, Gregory, how much and how fast the world is changing," Dermot Bane said dramatically. Imagine Mary and Bridget married to Blacks? Then changing the course of the discussion he asked Gregory:

"Any one to see you in hospital?"

"No, not a soul, barring yourself and your Mrs —"

"Just look at that?" Dermot Bane said, mildly surprised. "I thought you were a popular man in the parish; I thought, mind you, that people would be queueing up to see you?"

"Well, dammit, if I am popular, and they were queueing up, they must have been invisible or else I was unconscious or blind, for I did not see them! If I were T. N. T. O'Blarney, T.D., or Senator Palladinus MacPoughin, or the Archdeacon of Drummullan, they would be there and seen to be there. When you are poor and desolate, and no way influential, who cares? People are interested in themselves and in what they can get out of you. It is not what they can give you, it is what you can give them —"

"Very true, Gregory," Dermot Bane said in agreement with his friend's assertion. "That is human nature. It has been that way ever since the Fall. You have often heard the poem:

'At the death of a beggar no comets are seen;
But the Heavens blaze forth at the death of a Queen!'

"Without a doubt the same applies to poor and common men like you and me. When we are ill, who is to see us? And when we are dead, who is to bury us? When you see a small funeral going down the street towards the chapel or the graveyard, you may be certain that the corpse is that of a poor man? You remember what Jesus Christ said about the rich man having little chance of entering Heaven?"

"I do indeed," Gregory said.

"With big funerals and pleasures of various descriptions, the rich obtain their rewards. When you are a poor man you stand a better chance of getting to Heaven, but meanwhile you have to lead a lonely and bitter existence here on earth —"

"That is the way," Gregory agreed stoutly. Adding: "Everything in moderation, I suppose? You had a murder down your way last month?"

"Aye so, bad business it was! It has given the district a rowdy name, I can assure you." Dermot Bane complained. "I suppose you read all about it in the newspapers? Mind you, Gregory, there was not much about the murder in *The Lough Swilly Echo*, or, for that matter, in any of the Donegal newspapers. Those reporters are sensible fellows: They have a sense of proportion and respect the feelings of relatives belonging to the murderer and her victim. *The News of the World!* — that is one piece of gossip I dislike because it will publish any thing middling, especially if it has anything to do with sex or murder —"

"Och the hospital was full of talk," Gregory told his friend as he threw another shovelful of coal on the fire. "The television and radio were on goodo, and patients who knew where I was from, asked me questions galore; dammit it all, I could not tell them a lot; they knew more than I did. What happened at all? Did she go out of her latitude, or what? There was this nurse called MacDaid — a budding writer of detective stories and other thrillers, who wanted facts. Says she to me when she was making my bed:

" 'Mr MacGarvey, you come from the Ballymullan district?'

" 'I do, Nurse,' says I.

" 'You knew, I suppose, the characters involved?'

" 'Vaguely', I replied.

" 'I have a note book here in my pocket —'

"I cut in before she could put another question: 'I will not give you details now but I promise to do so the very minute I go home . . .'

"She is a clever joker. You could not ask for a kinder nurse. I would like to send her a full account of the murder because I may have to go back to hospital in six months' time for a check-up, and it would be good to know I would be attended by a nurse who appreciated a small favour; you understand?"

"I do of course. Aye so. She would not be slow in showing you her gratitude for having helped her off on a literary career —"

"The very thing," Gregory said, nodding significantly. "She would be all over me, and dammit, a bachelor of my time-of-day needs friends in the right quarters, and something to look forward to besides the graveyard!"

"Aye so," Dermot Bane confirmed lightly. "I am not one for disappointing an old friend, or for keeping him from doing his favourite nurse a good-turn; I will tell you all I know — which, unfortunately, is not much, and, then again, it is too much; I wish the like had never happened in our parish. You know what I mean, Gregory?"

"I do indeed."

"I was there. I arrived on the scene shortly after the report of the fatal shooting had gone abroad . . ."

Dermot Bane finished the story and blew his nose into his handkerchief.

"Care for a cup of tea?" Gregory asked his friend as he got up shakily to fill the kettle and to slice bread.

"Aye so, I would indeed, Gregory. When we used to cut peat and turf in the bogs years ago, and you used to make tea, and boil the eggs, we thought you were the best tea-maker in the parish, and that is the truth!"

"Ach, we had grand times then cutting and handling turf. It was sore work — hard on the old back — but the bog was a grand place in which to work up an appetite —"

"You could eat a man off his horse and then eat the horse," Dermot Bane said, remembering with pleasure how it was when they were young and carefree.

"Ach, God be with those days; we will never see them again," Gregory said regretfully. "It was great to be young!"

"Aye so."

"Do you think they will hang her?" Gregory speculated about the fate of the murderess. She had shot her boy-friend.

"They might and they mightn't. According to St Colmcille's prophecy, no man from that part of Donegal will ever be hanged for murder —"

"But she is a woman! There is a vast difference: did Colmcille say anything about women being exempt from the rope, too?" Gregory said, thoughtfully.

"No, you are correct, I do not think he did, troth," Dermot Bane admitted astonished and struck with foreboding for the fate of the murderess.

They were thoughtful. After a lengthy silence Dermot Bane spoke:

"I heard her solicitor, Osbourne MacWilliam, is going to submit a plea of insanity, when her trial comes up for hearing next month, in Letterglinchey. He is a very clever solicitor; and you may be assured she will not be hanged but committed, for life, to some mental asylum or prison —"

"They would be wise to keep her out of circulation; put her where she will not be shooting fellows she fancies!" Gregory said gravely.

"Aye so!" Dermot Bane agreed.

When Gregory had made the tea, and the two old cohorts were seated round his unpolished table, he asked Dermot Bane where his wife and daughters were going to spend their summer holidays.

THE LAZY BEAUTY

Francis O'Mara was crazy about Jane MacNeill.

Jane was a rare beauty. The single men of the parish had all paid court to her, and had asked her father for her hand in marriage. She was such a remarkable beauty, and had such a captivating personality, that many respectable married men found their darling wives luridly dull after they had been more than five minutes in her company.

Jane's parents doted on her — her wish was their imperative. Her mother was a very ambitious woman, and hoped by means of her gifted daughter to form an alliance with some very old, wealthy, and influential family. She would not let Jane touch a dirty plate, nor wash a vest, nor darn a pair of socks, nor do any other menial task lest perhaps her delicate and attractive little hands should look soiled; not that Jane needed encouragement to take life easy: she was bone lazy!

Francis was a fine, upstanding, youthful fellow. He was a brush manufacturer. Gardening was his main hobby; and he loved to spend hours in his three large gardens. That was before he met Jane!

Francis fell in love with Jane at first sight. She was eighteen at the time. Francy, as Jane affectionately called him, was then twenty five. To his immense joy his love was reciprocated — much to the regret of her family.

Her family disapproved of Francis on one important premise: Poverty.

"Francis O'Mara," Mrs. MacNeill told her daughter, "is a poor boy. What happiness could he bring into your life, my dear?"

"O, I like him, Mama, because he is gay, sincere, courteous, and is not spoiled like other fellows. He loves me for myself — and not for any selfish reason —"

"All men are selfish!" Mrs. MacNeill interposed. "Why, Jane, he is illiterate? And besides he moves in the wrong social circles. You would be a slave married to that brush manufacturer, who is little better off financially and socially than a carpenter, or a tailor. I am surprised at you. I brought you up to respect my judgement — you know I have your best interests at heart, your happiness dear — you know that, do you not, dear?"

"Mama you have not my true happiness at heart. I love Francy; he loves me. He is generous and light-hearted and handsome and smells nice, too, not like those horrible creatures Dada brings here; they disgust me. O, Mama, if you knew how happy I am when Francy is around you would not be saying those unpleasant words about him . . ."

Mrs. MacNeill relented remotely, hoping to please her daughter; but she still disliked the idea of her daughter being so gullible as to allow herself become infatuated with a brush manufacturer whose family lacked substance. She hoped that Jane would tumble to her folly before long; otherwise plans might go wrong entirely!

One evening, when Jane and Francy were walking down a path in the woods near her home, Francy looked into Jane's hazel eyes, and, seeing the whole world there, he asked her to be his helper and bed-mate for the rest of his life. With the moon rising about Slieve Snacht, and casting shadows on the rippling waters of Lough Swilly, Jane was powerless to say any thing else but 'yes'.

"Yes, yes, yes!" she replied quickly. She whispered silly love words in his ear. She kissed him on the cheek, saying:

"You will have to speak with Dada, tonight, my darling."

"Do I have to?" Francis asked, forgetting that Jane was not yet of age and that it was still a cherished convention in her social group.

"I am afraid so, darling. Come! Dada is not a wolf, he will be nice to you; he will give his consent, you will see," Jane said reassuringly.

"I suppose I shall if I must. But only for you, Jane, my

sweet flower of May!"

Jane pressed his hand and kissed him on the mouth. They walked on leisurely down the path in the direction of her house. A light was burning in the library.

"Dada is reading," Jane told Francis when they had drawn near the house. "Come in, he is on his own!"

She led the way across the hall. She knocked, and entered the room. Her father was sitting with his back to the door; he was reading a respectable edition of 'Fanny Hill'. Startled, he turned and looked over his shoulder when they walked over to his desk, holding hands.

"I am sorry Dada for disturbing your reading. Could Francy have a minute of your precious time? It is . . . it is very important1 —"

"Yes, yes, all right, all right, make it brief young fellow, make it brief young —"

"Thank you Dada," Jane said, delighted. She kissed him on the cheek and left the library, leaving the two men staring like crooks at each other.

Francis was confused and began to shake at the knees. He did not quite know how to begin.

"Well! Well! Well, young fellow, young fellow, do not stand there looking like a pillar of salt, say what is on your mind and then get out, get out!" Mr. MacNeill commanded fiercely.

Suddenly Francis was vexed. His manliness was stung by the old man's ill humour.

"Sir, I have come to ask you for your daughter's hand in marriage!"

Francis spoke the words calmly and formally and with such a degree of self-possession that the old man was at a loss what to say. It was his intention to say 'no', but instead he said:

"Of course, young fellow, of course, young fellow, of —"

Mr. MacNeill stopped talking abruptly and pulled himself up and stood looking across the desk at Francis — surprised at his own words of consent. Knowing that it was now too late to rectify his error, he added:

"When Jane is twenty-one mind, when Jane is twenty-one mind, when —"

Francis cut him short:

"Thank you, Mr. MacNeill. That is all for the moment." Then he walked out of the room and saw Jane listening at the keyhole.

"Well? Well?" she demanded; perhaps she had not heard clearly what was said after all.

Francis laughted. Jane laughed too.

"Dada has given his consent," Jane said joyously when Francis told her what transpired. She joined her hands above her heaving bosom and stroked her chin with the points of her fingers. "That is grand, darling."

"Yes, but" . . . Francis was shaking again at the knees. "He says we must wait until you are twenty-one!"

"Do not fret, darling; I will get to work on Dada in the morning. Come, we will tell Mama . . ."

Mr. MacNeill did not change his mind about his daughter having to wait until she became of age before marrying Francis O'Mara.

Francis was wild with anxiety meanwhile. He believed that the old man was trying to get his daughter to change her mind by throwing her at his favourites, and he spared no expense in keeping Jane travelling abroad in the company of eligible bachelors, who were also wealthy, influential, and madly in love with her too. However Jane held out, principally to spite her father; obstinacy was part of her personality.

Francis worked twelve hours a day, six days a week. He built a bungalow, wore the latest fashions, and engaged the local school master to give him private tuition. Instead of fruits, flowers and trees, he concentrated on cultivating wealthy and influential friends. Love for a woman had driven him to do things he would not have dreamed of doing for a reward of a million pounds.

Then came the day when Francis brought Jane down the aisle on his arm. The wedding march was playing, Jane was smiling — her exquisite smile, friends and well-wishers were waving and cheering; outside, the sun seemed to be also smiling, and the sweet smell of lilac was mingled with the cool refreshing early June breeze.

"Oh, is it not absolutely enchanting?" one fat lady said loudly to her friend after she had kissed the bride and shaken hands with the groom.

"Yes, quite; very lovely . . ."

Francis thought he was in the middle of a most exquisite dream; and if it were a dream, he did not want to awake. He saw himself sitting beside Jane at their wedding reception in her father's mansion; he could see the two of them leading the floor — dancing the waltz; he saw them setting out on their honeymoon and the cheering guests, and hear them uttering silly and embarrassing words of farewell; and, finally, he could see himself alone with her in some gaily decorated, carpeted hotel room in the seaside resort of beautiful Bundoran . . . yes, it was a heavenly dream . . . And it was coming true!

Francis knew he was the envy of the whole parish. Since their return from an exotic honeymoon, Jane had been busy giving parties, and attending parties in her honour. At first he was not put out — such indulgence was the usual run of things, but, as time passed, and more and more parties were being held in his house, and he was constantly being dragged away to functions, his business begin to be adversely affected. He tried to talk Jane into leading a quieter life. She did not quite understand his position at the beginning, but, when he had told her of the money he was borrowing in order to provide for her spree of extravaganza, she was very nice about every thing, and said she would cut out all unnecessary expenditure — if he would promise to engage another maid.

Francis learned with amazing rapidity that Jane had many faults. Everybody, including himself, he knew, had faults; and if people were not prepared to be patient and forgiving, what kind of a world would this be at all? But there was a limit to everything!

Towards the end of the second year of their marriage Francis dismissed Jane's two maids despite her protests; he was now heavily in debt and creditors would not lend him any more money. He refused to consider asking her father for financial assistance as she had suggested.

"How do you expect me to live without maids?" Jane said when they were going to bed one night. "Who is going to do all the work involved in running this house?"

"We are!" Francis told her bluntly. She had to hear the truth of the situation some time and she had to be given notions of practical economies.

It was a brutal shock for her and she ran off in a huff to sleep for the night in the spare bedroom on the far end of the hall. Francis felt sad about having upset her; but what else could he do — except wait on her, hand and foot?

At the end of their third year of marriage Francis was spending more time attending to the wants and needs of his wife than working in his little factory. Business was gradually getting worse, creditors were tightening their reins, and Jane was showing no signs of providing him with an heir.

Francis realised, at last, that he was no longer the envy of the parish: Not that his wife was any less beautiful or charming, but because she would not do one hand's turn of house-work! She still insisted on getting breakfast in bed, being helped to dress, and on having her room and the whole house scrubbed, polished, and brushed by hand — Francis' hand! He knew the matter had gone too far, that some radical solution was required.

Francis was in a crowded public-house one evening having a quiet drink with a few close friends, when one of them, the worse for drink, said:

"When is young Francy O'Mara coming along?"

It was a vulgar question to ask. Francis knew his friend meant no harm by it; however he guessed his friend's palaver was an echo of the talk that was current in the parish.

Francis felt embarrassed at first; then he grew angry and disgusted with his wife: She had reduced him to the position of a flunkey and hand-maid. That evening he came home to her, drunk. When she gave out to him for having been late for supper, which he was to have cooked, he struck her, adding:

"You lazy lout! That is what you are! If it were not for me having kept you clean, and the house clean, you would be living in filth. And, another thing: When are you going to give me a son? — or a daughter!"

Francis was sarcastic on purpose. Jane was alarmed and hurt by his words and violence; she went into her bedroom and shut the door.

"Lazy lout," he kept shouting through the door. "Sitting

all day long before the mirror painting your face, finger-nails, brushing your hair, and looking at and admiring your image in the glass . . . Lazy lout . . . dirty slut. Lazy lout, dirty slut!" he shouted several times. "Prude! I am the laughing stock of the whole parish . . ."

During a lull in his shouting, Jane told him that perhaps he himself was the partner at fault: that perhaps he would never have an heir because he was sterile and therefore unable to father a child.

This accusation threw Francis into another violent fit.

"Do not cod yourself, Madam; for I can tell you, I sired a youngster when I was working in Scotland . . ."

Francis lay down on a couch in the kitchen and fell fast asleep. He made breakfast for himself, alone, the next morning; and after he had put a few shirts, socks, and under-wear into an old suit-case, he walked down the road deter-mined never to return to his lazy beauty.

"Lazy lout, dirty slut, prude!" Francis said to himself when he was a mile down the road. He stopped, turned about, and looked back at his domain. "There will be barnicles on your arse," he muttered (directing his talk to Jane), before you see my face again, Madam!"

Then he walked on down the road more firm in his resolve than before.

When Francis did not return home after an absence of one week, Jane was very upset; and she sent word to her father and mother, asking the former to come and take her home.

When a whole year had passed, and Francis had not written nor returned home, Jane was finally convinced that she had been deserted by her husband. In the meantime, creditors had filed a petition of bankruptcy and the estate was put into the hands of an official receiver. Jane wondered where he was, or what he was doing, and she kept thinking about what Francis had said when they quarrelled; she regretted many things and prayed for forgiveness and the return of her husband.

Years passed. Jane was no longer the most beautiful girl in the parish; unhappiness had aged her, prematurely; she rarely smiled and her hearty laughter was never heard after her husband went away.

One day she had a visitor — her favourite cousin, Robert John MacGavern. When he entered her room she was sitting in front of the mirror admiring her pale and embittered reflection in the glass. They were closeted for over an hour. When Robert John had taken his leave, Jane ran into the library, sobbing; she cried on her father's shoulder.

"What is the matter, dear? What is the —"

"It is awful, Dada," Jane roared, crying. "Cousin Robert John told me Francy is living with a woman in Scotland."

"What? What? What?"

"Yes, Dada! Francy is living with a dirty slut in Perthshire. It is horrible. I am shamed for life: Imagine my husband living in adultery! And I am partly responsible for his degradation and my own. My God, Dada, what am I to do?" Jane cried bitterly. When she had calmed down, she told her father what Robert John had related during his visit:

"One day last month, when Johnny O'Mahan and Charley MacHarkin were travelling through the Highlands in search of work, they called to the door of a large farm-house, not far from the town of Perth, and asked for a job.

"A woman came to meet them at the door. They told her they were looking for work. She said she had a good man looking after her farm, that she did not need extra hands. They were thirsty and asked her for a drink of water; while she was filling jugs with water, Charley leaned against the door-frame and saw Francy sitting at the dinner table beside two little girls."

"Did Francis speak to Charley? Did Francis —"

"No, Dada! Francy looked at Charley and Charley looked at Francy, but neither man spoke. When the woman took back her jugs, Charley and Johnny thanked her and went off minding their own business," Jane said.

"Charley and Johnny jumped to the conclusion that Francis is living with the woman! A reasonable assumption, but damned scandalous; damned scandalous. Frankly, I do not believe Francis O'Mara would prefer a slut to my decent daughter; decent daughter. It would be out of character for him to do such a thing and I think you can disregard —"

"It is awful, Dada," Jane said, hoping her father was right

about Francis. "I am scandalised before the whole parish; I have failed you and Mama —"

"Do not worry dear; do not —"

"I have disgraced you and Mama; it is awful, Dada; it is awful," Jane said and sobbed more bitterly than before. When she returned to her room she sat before the mirror drying her tears. Then there was a gentle knock on her door. she opened it and found one of her maids standing there, holding a letter. It was from Francis. With trembling hands and deep emotion Jane read his short and semi-literate scribble.

When she had read his letter five times her eyes sparkled with a new light and a sweet smile broke upon her lips. Then she ran down the stairs shouting joyfully, her parents were surprised at her sudden change of humour.

"Francy darling has written a sweet letter to me," Jane said and showed them his letter. "He says he loves me; he begs my forgiveness for the things he said and for having run away from his responsibilities; further, he says he never fathered a child; that his relationship with the woman for whom he works is entirely honourable; that she is a widow by the name of Stuart; that he has money saved and wants me to come to him in Perth; that he has the use of a house attached to the farm; he also says the house is cosy and the countryside closely resembles Drumknock. 'Come to me my sweetheart', he says; 'let us start a new life together . . . Please write soon . . .' "

Jane was beside herself with happiness. "I shall scrub, cook and sew for you, my darling," she said to the wind as if it could carry her response to her Francy. "My darling Francy I am coming to you . . ." Instead of writing, and in spite of her mother's opposition, she packed her cases and sailed to Scotland.

A reunion took place three days later between husband and wife. The love they had once shared flamed higher than before and this made up for the years they had been separated. Jane became an entirely new kind of person because she worked vigorously to make their humble cottage look like a miniature castle, where there were no servants but one — herself. Francis was completely overwhelmed by her good intentions and hard work and begged her to take life easy but she laughingly disregarded his words of admonition and went on slaving for her farmer-husband.

Jane's laughter was heard once again and that sweet smile was seldom off her lips and Francis could not understand why he had been such a fool to desert his beautiful and charming and hard-working wife. Because Jane was unaccustomed to physical exertion her passion for providing their cottage with her own service began to undermine her health; she developed a serious heart condition and one day, less than two years after her arrival in Perth, her exertions brought on a heart attack in the evening of July 31, 1899.

Jane died in her husband's arms; her last words to him were: "My darling I have proved my love!"

Heartbroken, Francis O'Mara brought his wife's remains home to Ireland and had them interred in a grave-yard not far from the spot where he had asked Jane to be his wife less than twenty years before.

THE CRUEL MURDERER

I was horrified at seeing pups disposed off by drowning in the river when I was young.

This was a phobia; I think it originated one day when I was bathing in a streamlet and witnessed a neighbour named Neddy MacDaid drowning his dog.

Neddy MacDaid was over eighty, but he was still strong of body and lucid of mind. We called him Old Neddy. He was not a cruel man. Yet he put his dog named Jack to death for killing sheep in the Ucterlinn Hills.

As I stood watching Old Neddy burying the dog, he told me that pirates executed their prisoners by tying their hands behind their backs and making them walk the plank blindfold.

"Horrible," I said in disgust.

"Their prisoners drowned and that was that," Old Neddy said with emphasis, "if the sharks did not have them first."

"Very cruel," I exclaimed and shuddered.

"You complain of my cruelty in having drowned a good-for-nothing sheep-killing-dog! You said drowning prisoners was horrible. What would you say about killing a pregnant servant-girl by drowning?" Old Neddy asked earnestly.

"Horribly cruel, Neddy," I told him with another shudder. "Who would do such a think?" I added.

Old Neddy stopped digging and looked at me intently. "You are young and innocent to the wicked ways of the world. I may shock your delicate feelings, Dano, by telling you a true story about the villainous deed of drowning a pregnant servant girl. What could be much worse? Listen here to me. Not far from where you are standing there is the ruins of what was once a prosperous establishment — no wonder, my God, it is in ruins today! — which I shall not name for charity sake, wherein a poor, ignorant and unfortunate servant girl was hired in days gone by."

I stared at Old Neddy as he rested his elbow on the shaft of his spade.

"The gentleman of the Mansion noticed that the servant girl's belly was gradually getting bigger and realised eventually that she was in the family way. He watched her closely. He had a suspicion that, since she only visited the local church and shop and post office, and stayed home at night, his son was having illicit relations with her. The gentleman's son was twenty and as sly as a fox.

"One day, when he was alone in the Mansion with his son, he asked his son if he was responsible for the servant girl being pregnant. His son, knowing how much the gentleman hated sexual immorality, and being of a cowardly disposition, stoutly denied having carnal knowledge of their servant girl.

" 'In that case,' the gentleman declared, 'we must avoid a scandal by disposing of her quietly.'

The son thought his father, who was generous, pious, and an avid reader of the bible, intended dismissing her and sending her back to her own people, with a lump sum to help provide for her confinement and loss of earnings, before her condition became common knowledge in the parish.

"Late one moonlit night the gentleman and his son and the servant girl went down to the Bay to gather seaweed for manuring the coming year's crop of potatoes. They carried a spade, a fork, a grape, and a grapple.

"The gentleman bade the servant girl wade knee-deep in the water in order to collect floating seaweed whilst he himself and his son rolled up the legs of their trousers. Although it was the month of March, when the water is still bitterly cold, she entered the sea without protest, so obedient was her mild nature.

"She was collecting seaweed when the gentleman delivered a blow to the head which knocked her flat on her face in the icy water; then he sat upon her back in order to keep her submerged in the sea; she struggled for a while; however, before his son understood what was happening the servant girl was dead or beyond human aid.

"Pushing aside his son, who had gone to the assistance of the servant girl, the gentleman commanded: 'Give me a hand with her. We must bury his load of filth.'

"The son was thunderstrock. He stood there like a rock, unable to move for terror. When he got his voice he said: 'Father,' he cried bitterly, 'God Almighty, you have killed her?'

"The gentleman did not reply immediately. Instead, he caught her by the legs and dragged her ashore.

" 'Come, come, come along boy, get a move on, get a move on, my boy, we have to work speedily; we must get her out of sight before neighbours come along and see her corpse and get us into a spot of bother with the authorities,' the gentleman warned. 'Start digging, make haste.'

"Without further comment the two men, who had carried the corpse to a hollow between two sand dunes, began to dig a deep grave. They worked in silence. When the grave was dug, and they had placed her corpse carefully in position, the gentleman took a bible from his pocket and began to read in a low voice; his son shed tears as he uttered a mental prayer. When they finished filling and camouflaging the grave they returned to their task of gathering seaweed as if nothing out of the usual had occurred.

"In time, word went abroad that the servant girl had quit the Mansion and questions were asked, such as: 'She is not at home, where is she? When was she last seen? What could have made her disappear?'

" 'Miss Jenny disappeared one night when we were gathering seaweed,' the gentleman would say casually when questioned. 'Upon our return, she was no longer to be seen, high up or low down . . . Perhaps she has gone to America? Come to think of it,' the gentleman would say 'Jenny did mention her wish to visit the United States, where she has relatives. Perhaps I should not say this,' he would add confidentially, 'but a small sum of money was stolen from my office the night she went away.' The matter was the talk of the parish for weeks. It seemed to be taken for granted that she went abroad and, after a few months her name ceased to be mentioned, life going on as before. At the Mansion she was replaced by a much older and wiser servant girl as a safety precaution, but the son was beyond caring about any thing: Within a year of Jenny's murder he went out of his mind and drowned himself."

"And the gentleman," I asked, "What happened to him?"

"God's justice did not catch up with him in this world," said Neddy shaking his head regretfully, 'He lived to the age of ninety and died peacefully in his sleep." Then Neddy went on with his work and I went home sorrowfully.

Never again did I bathe in the streamlet where Neddy drowned his dog.

THE SERGEANT'S DAUGHTER

I was almost man-big before I saw Sergeant O'Lanagan in civies. I remember it was the evening of a fine Sunday in June, and the Corpus Christi Day procession had just been brought to a close with prayers in Drummullan. I was standing a few feet away from the Chapel door among a crowd of men when the Sergeant went by, accompanied by a child.

"That is the Sergeant in civilian clothes," said Neil Mac-Edward with emphasis.

Neil was a slightly built, black bearded fellow from down the country. He was standing next to me when he made reference to the Sergeant's dress.

"It is unusual," I replied, "to see the Sergeant in plain clothes. He goes every where in uniform."

"Jakits aye, he does," Neil confirmed; "you are on the mark! You would think he was born in it! Course, there are some advantages to be gained from wearing the uniform at all times."

Neil went on in a philosophical manner. "When the Guards are wearing the old blue uniform, they are admitted free of charge to sports, football matches, race meetings; travel free of charge on public transport; and avoid arrest during fights in public houses, at fairs, and in dance halls — you can imagine the possibilities?"

"Too true, I do, Neil." said I.

"Our friend, the Sergeant, being a clever character, seldom ventures outside his own door in plain clothes. Besides, the uniform is warm, gives good wear and is government property. Why not use public property to the maximum —"

"Yes, yes, I see your point, Neil." I told him.

Neil could be satirical be times. "There are no flies on the Sergeant," I added after reflection. "Where is he from, Neil?" I heard him speaking to his companion when he went past; and, since his accent was difficult to understand, I wanted to know which part of Ireland spoke his dialect.

"He is an 'Up-the-Country-Man'," Neil asserted. "Leitrim or Roscommon, I believe; so Master O'Hallow tells me!"

"How long has he been here in Drummullan, Neil?" I asked casually. "Is he coming near retiring age?"

"Well, damn the bit of him — he is still a young man. He cannot be more than fifty-five or fifty-six — they retire at sixty-five, I understand."

Neil was knowledgeable.

"Has he much learning?" I asked Neil. I was interested to know what standard of education was required for admittance to the force. I had a notion of joining them, if I could push my height up to five feet nine inches, the minimum height for entry.

"National school education!" Neil told me frankly. "I heard he was promoted for bravery; he caught a murderer in some place up the country where he was stationed last. I do not think he would get promoted through learning — he is no scholar and has but a small amount of book learning, like you know. No, nothing like that; a brave man surely, but —"

"Tough man, the Sergeant; I would not like to get on the wrong side of his anger," I commented. "He is a strong man and must be fourteen stone, if he is an ounce.

"Aye; and would you look at the height of him, he is six feet to the inch," Neil announced with conviction.

"That cannot be true," I countered, "because there was only one man an even six-foot, and that was Jesus Christ, Himself!"

Neil looks me straight in the eye and says he: "That may be your opinion; after all you read a lot, but I heard the Sergeant tell Vince MacPolland, that, when he was a young man entering the Guards he was six-feet; the Sergeant is a truthful man, he would not lie about a simple thing like his height —"

"But he could have been mistaken?"

Neil spat on the ground and shook his head with conviction. He was wearing a cap.

"Nice cap!" I told Neil when I noticed his headgear. I looked at it admiringly and this pleased him to some considerable extent. He was vain in small matters and I wanted to change the subject.

"'Tis in sang. Joe, my brother, who lives in Glasgow, sent me a parcel of them last Christmas."

"We will be going home," I suggested. Neil and I started down the Chapel avenue.

It was a lovely avenue. The Canon kept the walks and avenues and hedges in splendid shape. The scent from the blossoms and flowers was refreshing and reminded me of a happy episode in my childhood days, in the country, years before.

"The Sergeant is well-off," Neil explained. "He could live in the sleeping quarters of the Barracks but prefers to live with his family, in a private house at the end of Coast Court Row. So there you are now."

"I know he is married," I told Neil pertly. "I think he has a daughter attending the dances?"

"He has indeed," Neil confirmed. "I suppose, Dano, that you do be dancing her now and then." He looked at me suspiciously.

"It is possible I have had the pleasure —"

"Aye! — sure you would be well fixed there, so you would indeed." Neil looked at me closely and wistfully, and advised: "You should treat her like a lady ought to be treated by a gentleman. I would not like to be in the shoes of the fellow who would be trifling with her affections . . ."

I did not absorb the remainder of the sentence because I blushed and became somewhat confused. I was very sensitive to any suggestion, or insinuation, that I would treat a lady in a dishonourable manner. Seeing my embarrassment Neil said jokingly:

"Sure, 'tis only codding I am; sure I know 'tis Chivalry himself you are, Dano. I was only speculating. I see you do have eyes for her — if I am not mistaken?" Neil expounded. "Sure I wish be times I were a young man, about your age, and in the running; sure I would be after her myself and no better man. Sure 'tis only natural; and what is natural, is not sinful . . ."

Talk about sex always upset me in those days, because I was basically ignorant of the facts of life to an appalling degree; in any event, I had some horror of making a girl pregnant, and, any insinuation that I might be misbehaving myself in the company of a respectable girl, sent a shudder of panic and shame and blood to my head. I changed the subject instantly.

"The Sergeant's son is a good footballer!" Neil was a keen fan; by using this ruse about football I hoped to be on sure ground.

"Which son? The Sergeant's eldest son, who is away in College studying for the priesthood? — or the amadan of a Jose fellow, who is going to school in Letterglinchey?" Neil was a tiny bit annoyed.

"Jose! I did not know he has a son going on for the priesthood." I was not well informed on social affairs in Drummullan.

"Jose could not kick his own door properly even if he had a grip of its latch!" Neil said indignantly. "You must be a poor judge of footballers," he added gravely. "But the Sergeant's daughter has class and no mistake; there you have as good judgement as I have; that you have, you are no fool."

I tried once again to change the subject. "What do you think of the Sergeant, generally speaking. Do you think he is a good detective?"

"Ah! Dano, my old potato, he is like the rest of us, he has his faults. And pet hates and . . . I suppose you know what I mean?" Neil wondered.

"I do," I assured Neil, and I did not! I wanted to win his respect and admitting my ignorance might not be the most astute way of getting it.

"If the Sergeant likes you he would turn a blind eye, but if he should have a spite to you — now, by sang, you would better watch your step."

Neil sighed and took off his cap, scratched his unwashed head, blew his long nose at the roadside, wiped it with his finger and thumb, and cleaned his finger and thumb on the side of his trousers, and continued talking:

"I remember last year when he summoned Frank Mac-Quinn for not having cut his benweeds. The judge let Frank off with a caution, and the Sergeant was raging-mad. Last winter he finally found Frank in a spot. Frank was drunk while riding his bicycle without a light. The Sergeant served another summons 'pon Frank. The judge gave Frank a severe reprimand, saying: 'Mr MacQuinn, should you appear before me in the near future on a similar charge, or charges, I shall be compelled to fine you, and, if necessary, confine you. Do you hear me now?' Frank was frightened and solemnly promised to keep within the Law of the Land henceforward.

"Again the Sergeant was disappointed. At the next sitting of the District Court, the Sergeant had Frank up on no less than two serious charges: Not having a wireless licence and a dog licence. This was more than the poor old judge could stand; he fined Frank ten pounds; and, says he to Frank: 'Do not let me see you here again. It is a disgrace for you having tried to defraud the State of its lawful revenue. Either pay your just taxes or else do not keep a radio or a dog'. The judge was very annoyed. That evening Sergeant Michael O'Lanagan, G.S. was in the pick of humour; he was heard singing a rebel song as he went about the village in the course of duty!"

I knew Frank MacQuinn vaguely: He was a surly cur. I laughed — in fact, I roared with hilarity. I suppose my laughter was contagious because Neil, who saw only the serious side of life most of the time, chuckled.

When we had finished laughing and had regained our composure, Neil asked:

"Dano, did I ever tell you the reel about the Sergeant ordering Charles Big-John and Josephus Wild-Sherman out of the village one Sunday evening last year?"

"No; what was it all about, Neil?" I asked anxious to hear of the affair.

Neil seemed delighted that I had not heard of the reel, as he called it, and he began to relate it in his droll manner, while we walked along the road. A slight but warm breeze was blowing from the West and the crops swayed gently and a few grey cloudlets floated overhead and the sun was sinking behind the mountains.

"The Sergeant," Neil began, "was standing in the doorway of the barracks smoking his pipe and having a breath of fresh air when our two friends were passing on two new bicycles.

"Good evening, Sergeant," says your two friends.

"Good evening, boys," the Sergeant returned, pleasantly and saluted.

"About five minutes later your two friends came down the street again:

"Nice evening, Sergeant," says they smiling, and they saluted.

"Nice evening, thank God, boys," replied the Sergeant and he wondered why they were passing a second time in the same direction. When they had disappeared at the corner he asked someone standing nearby, what business were the boys doing in town, and was told that they were cycling around the village looking for young girls.

" 'What?' says the Sergeant astonished. 'Them two old buckoes? At home, in their beds, they ought to be, bad scrat to them!'

"When Charles and Josephus were passing the door of the barracks after having completed a third circuit of the village, the Sergeant's tamper could not be contained; he shouted:

" 'Get away home to Hell; do not let me see you passing here again this evening!'

"Your two friends agreed amongst themselves that it was a free country; but they were wise enough not to risk getting on the wrong side of the Sergeant by disregarding his order, and they went home in bad humour —"

"Good evening lads; nice weather," a man with an up the country accent said behind us. We were startled. It was Sergeant O'Lanagan on an old bicycle, and before we had time to recover from our astonishment, he disappeared at the next bend.

"I am surprised," Neil said, "at seeing the Sergeant riding down the country on a Sunday evening!"

"It is very unusual," I said in agreement.

"I am supposing he is keeping an eye about him for law-breakers and having a look at the crops and herds and the like of that; he will be minding to have his daughter settled on some prosperous farm!"

I flushed.

Neil looked slyly about him, at me, and chuckled again.

I was so flushed and confused by his pointed words that I did not know what to say; and in my confusion I asked Neil did he think there would be a good crop of potatoes next year!